THE WORMHOLE

THE WORMHOLE

STEVEN DALE MAHER

PALMETTO
PUBLISHING
Charleston, SC
www.PalmettoPublishing.com

Copyright © 2024 by Steven Dale Maher

All rights reserved

No portion of this book may be reproduced, stored in a retrieval system, or transmitted in any form by any means–electronic, mechanical, photocopy, recording, or other–except for brief quotations in printed reviews, without prior permission of the author.

Paperback ISBN: 9798822963412
eBook ISBN: 9798822963429

Part One

ONE

Ray awoke in a strange bed, at first unsure of where he was. And yet, it was here that he somehow knew he wanted to awake every morning for the rest of his life. He inched to get nearer to the warm body next to him but found he couldn't move. He was already so close to the girl in his arms that it seemed their two bodies were one, melted into a silent revolt against the rest of the outside world, as if in united protest of all the ugly and incalculable harm that the callous rulers of their innocent generation were making them suffer through.

The caress of her hair upon his cheek, the smell of her skin, the delicious wonder that perhaps some *god* was at work bringing two wandering, desperate lovers together in sacred-summer-salvation, a heaven-sanctified union of lonely waifs who've waited their entire young lives to leave the shadows of gray boredom behind and enter the scarlet sanctuary of love.

An old poem came to him, something about the real versus the unreal:

> In the middle of night
> I awake by her side

> and hope every time
> that it's her and not a dream.
> Only in morning light
> as she opens her eyes
> kissing me with sighs
> am I sure it's her and not a dream.

Dreams are what get us through the taunting tedium, the wan and yawn of an existence so hum-drum that we cry into our pillows at night, mused Ray, fantasizing of realities that we know can never exist, that we know are impossible. What is life without dreams, just a bloody, sloppy marrow of deer-meat, ingested and then later vomited into the sewers of helplessness and desolation. It's good to know this girl, this *savior,* is not a dream, though maybe she *is,* maybe life is just an illusion, a silly doodle on some god's frayed notepad, just a black-and-white hootenanny of useless and fruitless ideas, ludicrous concepts that are quickly abandoned, crumpled and tossed into a dented waste basket of obliviousness with all the other stupid dawdles and twaddles of a creator's imagination.

Jenna shifted ever so slightly, like a leaf stirred by a gentle, warmhearted breeze, then she sighed, just like in Ray's poem. Dream or no dream, this was exactly where he wanted to be, forever lying next to heaven, embracing paradise, breathing in the fragrant blossomy sweetness of his savior, never wanting to ever climb out of this holy of holies' bed.

Then she delicately and daintily turned to face him, opening wide her maple-colored eyes in all their shimmering glory, two unfolding tulips greeting the morning sun, ready to be smiled at, ready to welcome whatever the day had in store for them. The silvery voice of her eyes said, "Hello, darling!" and his own eyes replied, "Good morning, dear!" and their lips met in thirsty kiss, curious tongues creeping and crawling inside each other's mouths, tasting the intoxicating 'nectar of destiny' that nourishes true love.

The first ruby rays of sun whispered through the windowpane, a single faint star still visible in the glimmering crystal dome of a well-meaning sky that didn't want to insult the shrinking night while at the same time sympathetic to the growing day. The sky believed that night and day should not fight but instead wave peacefully at each other in passing, like two armies weary of battle, hoping to return to their respective resting places until each was ready to re-emerge in proud uniform, armored for duty.

The girl arose from the bed, her naked body not showing even one hint of self-consciousness, her tanned calf-muscles flexing and dancing at every poetic step as she glided into the blushing bathroom.

A moment later she coaxed, "Join me in the shower?"

Ray could hear the whistling of the water nozzle and the trysting of the inside-raindrops kissing the tub floor, their rapt rhyming sonance beckoning him to fairyland, to come and play within the toy-room of her glittering, golden body, to again taste and smell and savor the amber ambrosia and minty manna of her fragrant flesh, to suckle at the breast of Aphrodite, slide into the rapturing maze of Venus' fountainhead.

But Ray's own insecurities, his prejudices against his own body, his chagrinned embarrassment of his masculine shortcomings, his fear of not being perceived as a 'model of virility', kept him from *leaping* out of bed into the judging daylight, racing to fairyland where the most beautiful girl he'd ever met awaited.

Sure, they'd made love the night before but clever darkness had shielded his imperfections, wine had given him the brazen courage to romance a girl that sober he didn't *deserve* to lie with. She had said she liked the hair on his chest. That made him feel good. But then other girls had said that, and he'd eventually lost *them*. Lost them *all*. Romantic relationships were like milk, they all came with an expiration date, and whatever was left in the carton when the kissing stopped was poured down the sink, to be flushed into the dismal sea of broken dreams where no one can hear them scream.

He looked at his wristwatch, it was half past eight.

"No, I'll take a raincheck," he called back.

A *raincheck?* How charming was *that?* he thought. Yeah, that was the brilliant response of a 'Casanova', a 'Romeo', a *model of virility.*

There was no sound from the bathroom but happy raindrops continuing their enchanted journey across the wonderland of her naked body, a journey *he* should be enjoying, thirstily drinking every last luscious drop of water perched on taut brown nipple, every drop hiding inside a mysterious, inscrutable magical cave which lullabied, "Enter, pilgrim, pink delights and crimson sights you encounter within will insure you never want to leave!" A fool is born every minute and a mountain of regret rises higher and higher into a moron's unsympathetic sky.

He dressed and called out, "Ring you tonight at 6:30?"

There was no answer but the constant pitter-patter of water drops plinking the shower floor and the taunting gurgle of missed pleasure going down the bathtub drain, warm pleasure forever forfeited, forever lost.

TWO

"Sirloin steak and kill it, BBQ OTS!" yelled Alexander.

"Heard!" Ray yelled back, "but 86 the broccoli, sub carrots."

Richard clipped a chit on the rail. "The 4-tops and the 6-tops are all full, I'm in the weeds out there. And to make things worse, I got some big-wig at table 12 ordering off the menu. Says he wants potatoes au gratin made *only* with gouda cheese."

"Can't do," Ray said, "got no gouda, I'll add cheddar, maybe he won't know the difference."

Assistant manager Ahmad rushed in. "The Mayor and his latest girlfriend are at 12, who's got 12?"

"I do," sighed Richard, "and he's a real pain in the ass!"

"I don't care *what* he is, his lunch bill is more than ya make in a month! Get out on the floor and get whatever he wants, smart alec!"

"Yes *Sir*, your highness!"

"Don't highness me or I'll have ya fillin' the salt shakers! Go, go, go!"

God, I hate working here, Ray thought to himself, unsure of any other career he was qualified for. He'd been slapping plates on the counter since he was nineteen, starting at IHOP, segueing to Denny's, then landing this better-paying gig at Michaelangelo's where the quality of food was superior but the in-house corporate B.S. was the same. And the assistant managers were all the same, too, heckling, hassling, huffy, hacky swell-heads all.

He reached into the low-boy where he always kept a bottle of Hennessy and poured a dollop into the free beer provided by Kenny O. the bartender. You don't get *this* at IHOP! he said to himself.

"Hey, Cookie, fire up a lobster for the Mayor," Richard requested, "he's out there throwin' more of the taxpayers' money away!"

"Heard," Ray answered, "be on deck in eight minutes."

Three

"That *pervert* in the front row is creeping me out!" nodded Cynane, "he keeps sticking his tongue out like he wants to *lick* me."

"Goes with the territory," yawned Jenna, "you gotta learn to avoid eye contact, honey. Once you look at these pigs, they get a hard-on and think they're in love."

"Yeah? This one can show his love by stickin' another five in my thong!"

Weekday morning hours at Morty's strip club were usually pretty slow. Just five or six middle-aged men wandering in at a time dressed in wrinkled and stained overcoats, most of them taking seats alone in the dim back rows where they hoped no one would notice the quick jerking motions going on inside their ulsters.

The slow pace gave the girls time to gossip and catch up on each other's business, though some girls were evasive about their lives outside 'the office'. These pretended that they had smart and handsome boyfriends who were going to marry them and *rescue* them from this whole nastiness of disgusting dirty old men ogling and goggling them onstage. But the truth was, most of them lived with ne'er-do-wells who gambled or sold drugs for a living, or worse, pimped them out to husbands cruising the avenues in their Toyota Corollas looking for a brief sexual respite from their dull, dreary married lives.

At noon, Morty usually barked at two or three of the girls.

"Hed out, swe'thearts, place is empty, I's losin' muny 'ere payin' yu bitches ta sit 'round in yer stinky thon's. Buts be sur' ta be ba'k by eight, owner tells me th' Mayor is bringin' sum out-a-town *politicos* in t'nite, it's al' hands on deck! Not yu, Jenna, I's wantsta talk ta ya!"

Inside his dingy cramped office, Morty motioned Jenna to a chair in front of his lop-sided desk. She removed the stack of old, fraying Gent and Penthouse magazines and tossed them toward a wheezing floor-fan doing its best to circulate the dust.

"What's on that bright mind of yours, bossman?" Jenna asked.

"Nuttin'," glared Morty, "jus' hopin' ya 'ad time fer a quik bejay darlin'."

"I don't do that anymore," Jenna snapped, "remember? You told me once I'd worked here a year you wouldn't ask me to touch that shrimpy thing again."

"But, angel, Annabelle's in Buf'lo at thet ba'lroom dancin' theng, jus' this once, baby-dol', huh?"

"It's not my fault that the only girl in this god-awful dump willing to touch that pitiful little pecker-wang went to stupid

Buffalo to waste her creep-tips entering a dance-a-thon that she's guaranteed to finish last in! Go blow your own damn self!"

It felt good to let off some steam, Jenna thought to herself, as she stormed out of Morty's office, slamming the door for good measure. Ever since Ray declined a morning shower with her, she had been *itching* to let some man have it. *Men,* she griped to herself, you let one bang you and then he trots off into the pasture like some silly *donkey* who pretends he's a *stallion,* the cure to all womankind! Who needs them?

What rocky, winding life-path takes a pause at a strip club? No little girl says a bedtime prayer that she wishes to become a stripper when she grows up. But clubs are full of wandering females resoling their hiking boots and pondering what their next move should be.

Jenna grew up with a single mom living in a one-bedroom flat above a liquor store, a diner's flashing blue neon *Open All Night* sign glaring grumpily up at the frayed yellow polyester curtains covering the cracked kitchen window. It wasn't Mom's fault little Jenna came home from school to an empty apartment. Mom worked two minimum-wage jobs to pay the rent and keep food on the table. If Jenna's homework didn't get done, it was because no one was there to make sure it *was.*

But it was Mom's fault that those few hours a day she *was* home saw a steady stream of down-and-out unemployed drifters and grifters stopping in to share Mom's bed for a night or two of *jollys.* From her temporary banishment to the front room couch, Jenna listened to bedspring squeaks and muffled shrieks, all the while whispering *it's all right, Teddy, Mommy's ok* to her one-eyed stuffed bear. Maybe from such sad surroundings girls grow up to be lap-dancers; maybe they don't.

FOUR

Jenna answered the phone on the fifth ring, and of course, it was Ray, wanting to know if he could take her to Arby's for a roast-beef sandwich. *Arby's?* she asked herself, I thought he worked at some fancy highfalutin restaurant. Why can't he take me *there*? Am I *that* cheap of a date? All I deserve for probably the best screw of his life is a greasy sandwich?

"Sure," she muttered halfheartedly, "pick me up at 7:30." I'll be waiting with bells on my toes, she felt like adding.

She took another long shower to wash off the grime of the strip-club, the lonely shower-drops once again racing down to greet and lovingly prowl through every silky nook-and-cranny of her body, surveying and mapping each mysterious creamy crevice like adventurous explorers seeking Shangri-la, as if to say, "Ray, you have no *idea* of the sights you're missing!"

As Jenna let the warm rivulets of water roll off her body, she started thinking about that whole para-legal thing. She'd been in her oats *that* day coming up with a whopper like that. She'd been running for the courthouse elevator door on the fourth floor and this silly-smiling guy already on the lift stuck out his arm and blocked the sliding door from closing. Once safely inside, Jenna gratefully smiled back a thank-you. Staring at the lit-up floor numbers as 4 faded to 3, Jenna could feel the heat of the man's sin-smoldering gaze. It was as if she was standing on the rim of a volcano, enduring the fierce, stifling blast of the scalding magma below.

Then he gently sent a cooling breeze her way, asking if she was an attorney.

"You look like one of those high-priced lawyers who represent celebrities and CEO's," he tried to joke.

Maybe she *did* resemble some defender of the rich and famous that day, dressed in high heels and pantsuit, her smartly coifed hair tied back in a neat corporate pony-tail. Truth was, she'd been subpoenaed into court to testify as a witness to a stabbing at Morty's. One of the wiggling *creeps* had pulled a knife on another creep and buried it in the pervert's thigh for trying to cop a feel.

After undergoing twenty minutes of questioning, the whole time Jenna encountering the knife-stabber's menacing 'whore, I'm gonna cut you for this' stare, she didn't feel in the mood for admitting to this stranger-elevator-door-holder that she was in fact an erotic dancer at a cheesy downtown strip-club.

"I'm actually a para-legal working an IRS case against a famous slum-lord," she lied.

Where did she come up with *that* one? No harm done, she had thought at the time, me and door-holder are just two ships passing in the night. And it's a big ocean, we'll never meet again.

Oceans *are* big, but ships often follow the same routes. Wasn't ten minutes later that both Jenna and Ray were in the same hamburger joint on Fifty-First, munching soggy French-fries and sipping too thin milk shakes at opposite corners of the dingy diner. They both approached the cash register to pay their tabs at the same time.

"Well, it's a small world, counsellor," teased Ray, "what brings *you* here?"

"Hello again, stranger," smiled Jenna, "love the watery milk shakes, and the soggy fries, too."

After paying their bills, turned out they were walking the same way, up Fifty-First to Jones, then east toward the tunnel. Jenna was actually kind of happy to have the company of someone who *seemed* like a decent guy compared to that knife-stabbing freak in the courtroom. They circled around the park, engaging in polite chit-chat, and as often happens when boy meets girl, hand found hand, smile found smile, and two lonely souls ended up sharing a bed.

FIVE

Jenna glanced at the Arby's menu and felt like ordering two of everything. Then the bill might've added up to *one* decent meal at Michaelangelo's, where she felt Ray *should've* taken her after the night in paradise she had given him. What's *wrong* with men anyway, they think they can just nab a girl's most prized possession and then pay her back with a roast-beef sandwich?

"I think I'll try the Double Beef 'n' Cheddar," Ray smiled.

Wow, four whole dollars, thought Jenna, Mr. Money Bags! Okay, she said to herself, calm down, it's not *his* fault he's cheap, it's probably the way he was brought up. She started to feel sorry for him and ordered a single beef and cheddar for three dollars. At the table Ray began apologizing.

"Things are kinda tight right now, I don't get paid 'til Friday. Landlord raised the rent and my electricity bill almost doubled, damned utilities, storm knocks a few power lines down and they think they can just make the customers pay to replace 'em."

Okay, at least he said he was sorry, thought Jenna.

"Maybe when you're governor you can change all that," she teased, now completely calmed down and feeling warmhearted, like a lioness who feels sorry for a crying baby wildebeest she just seized by the neck and releases it to scramble back to it's mother.

"I'll take you out for a night on the town after I cash my paycheck, a big dinner at Michaelangelo's, then a show at Aristotle's nightclub, then a nightcap at The Dragoon! I'm sure you're used to finer surroundings when you're hangin' 'round with your lawyer friends."

Ah, there's that para-legal thing again, she sighed, gotta set that right. Eventually. Just not tonight. She was feeling too superior right now. Maybe next time they're together.

They walked arm in arm through the park again back to her place, the full moon dodging in and out behind the silver clouds, glaring at them, as if to say, I got my eye on you two, don't even *think* of trying to get out of making love tonight. They didn't.

SIX

Two days had passed before Ray saw Jenna again. He'd been working double shifts in the kitchen because Anson, the dinner chef had walked out during a fight with Ahmad over a slightly overcooked salmon fillet that a customer had sent back.

"This is the second time this month yuv sent out burnt salmon, Anson, why don't ya spend more time watchin' the stove and less time guzzlin' beer!"

"I'd *guzzle* less beer if yer boss didn't make the bar-jockeys serve me this *lite* crap! I'm the guy who keeps this whole fleapit goin' and he gives me the cheapest, watery horse-spit Budweiser ever made!"

"Yeah, maybe a *shoe* like yu ain't *worth* a pale-ale!" screamed a red-faced Ahmad.

"Who ya callin' a *shoe*, ya cookin'-school dropout. Ya know what they say about cookin' students who can't cook: they become assistant restaurant managers!" screamed back a redder-faced Anson.

Everything went downhill from there and ended up with the chef throwing his apron in the assistant manager's face, grabbing his Batman backpack and stomping out, *slamming* the back door loud enough for all the customers to hear. A spluttering and scuttering Ahmad raced to his office to call Ray at home.

When Ray answered, a panicked Ahmad squawked, "We got an *emergency* here, how quick can ya get down here? Jerkoff Anson left us high and dry, some customers are already walkin' out!"

Knowing the staff would fill him in on the scuttlebutt later, Ray replied, "Be there in ten."

When Ray got to Michaelangelo's, he saw customers slamming car doors and heading out of the parking lot, probably aiming for Armando's or The Pagoda or some other over-rated and over-priced chophouse.

Ahmad was still furious. "I'll make sure that overstuffed salmon-burner doesn't work another day in this town!" he spit.

"Say it, don't spray it," laughed Ray, "Anson's a good cook, he'll land a head chef's job within the week."

When he entered the kitchen, he found the dishwasher and the head busboy trying to put together a leek and potato soufflé.

"I got it from here, boys, thanks." Relieved, they went on back to washing platters and slicing French-bread. There were only three occupied tables left in the hushed dining-room, so Ray didn't feel like being in much of a hurry. He reached down into the low-boy and got his Hennessey out. Without waiting for a beer, he took two giant swigs.

The owner dropped in later that night on his way back from the opera, La bohéme, the story of a poor seamstress and her artist friends. Ray thought, where's the story of a poor cook and his waiter friends? Did Puccini ever compose *that* one, or did he leave that sad story for Abbott and Costello?

"I'll have Anson back here by nex' week," bragged the owner, "I'll giv' 'im a raise, he'll come."

Behind his back, Ahmad gave his boss the finger.

SEVEN

Ray cashed his paycheck at the payday lender on Fifth-Third, down by the railroad museum. These shysters' fees were totally absurd, he knew, but the credit union would give you only $100 up front until a check cleared. Giving Jenna a 'night on the town' would probably take more than that. Dinner, show and cocktail prices were going through the roof. That's what happens when you put Republicans in charge, he sneered. The economy goes into overdrive, 'full speed ahead and damn the torpedoes'. If a few million low-wage earners and welfare recipients get kicked to the curb, small price for making a few more billionaires! But he vowed not to dwell on scammy politics tonight. Let the masters of the universe *enjoy* their flim-flams and whim-whams. *Nothing* was going to bring him off this high he was on. He was in *Love*, the greatest feeling man or beast would ever have, the most glorious emotion in all the world, the most rewarding *gift* a god could grant a creature, lifting him or her to the pinnacle of happiness, to the euphoric summit of the mountain of ecstasy.

What kind of childhood grows a man to adopt such lofty and noble ideas of love? Ray grew up in a middle class setting, with two parents who respected each other and adored their two sons, Ray the oldest and Billy the youngest. There were picnics at the beach, visits to the zoo, camping vacations in the forest. As kids, Ray played little league, Billy played soccer, and both played on Pop Warner football teams. Dad helped Ray collect and sort baseball cards, took an avid interest in Billy's stamp collection, and helped both assemble model airplanes. Mom made both the boys nutritious school lunches, attended PTA meetings, and hosted Cub Scout get-togethers. An ideal middle class upbringing.

When it came time to discuss girls, *respect* was the primary adjective. Respect for their ideas, respect for their likes and dislikes, respect for their bodies.

"Don't ever make a girl do *anything* she doesn't want to do," Mom cautioned the boys.

"Cherish each girl you're with," added Dad, "one may become your lifelong partner and friend," and he kissed Mom.

EIGHT

Jenna had splurged and taken a cab home from a busier than usual afternoon of shaking and quaking her tight Snow-White ass in front of a whole squad of the city's finest, there to toast their precinct Captain's retirement. One of the tipsy homicide detectives had tipped her $100 to give Cap a private lap-dance. She wiggled and wriggled, slithered and slathered, squirmed and wormed all over that lucky lap. One of the patrolmen had to donate his long parka for his boss to wear back to the precinct to hide the lap stains.

Between the cop tips and all the fives the 'creeps' slid into her purple thong during her stage dances, Jenna was as flush as a back-alley craps winner. She rolled down the car window and let the cool evening city-air ruffle her hair, laying back against the head-rest and pondering why *every* day couldn't feel this good, why so many bleak, heartsore days just *plopped* in and *sat* on you like a carnival fat-woman who was waiting to be fed.

Ray had told her he was taking her to Michaelangelo's tonight and a little extra titty-money in her purse might come in handy if he ran short wining and dining her. She felt as good as a mouse-gorged cat and was ready to ride the stars like a rocket-ship. She didn't want *anything* to mar their grand adventure, to rain on their marmalade-parade. The cabbie dropped her off in front of her three-story walk-up and she smiled bright as a comet, tipping him $10, wishing him a 'happy good-night' and a 'may all your fares be high-tippers'. As she climbed the stairs, she even started whistling.

Ray showed up at Jenna's at seven with a huge smile on his face and a bouquet of red roses. He'd bought the flowers at a spot near the park on the way. As he jauntily traipsed the two blocks to the walk-up, it seemed every passerby either grinned or winked at him. *They* knew he was headed for an evening of crimson delirium-delicious bliss. The first stars were beginning to wake and twinkle their approval of this happy caballero on his way to amour's springtime round-up.

Jenna was still whistling as she opened the apartment door, and was both pleasantly surprised and annoyingly irritated as she accepted the roses. That was $20 *less* they now had for their grand adventure! Safely in a vase, the blooms looked on patiently as the two lovers' lips met in a both frenzied and long-lasting kiss. Ray kisses pretty good, Jenna thought, but his style could use some improvement, she'd hafta work on that. She slipped into her heels, grabbed her purse, and the adventure began.

Down the avenue they strode arm in arm like two entangled blackberry vines afraid to let go of each other lest they tumble into the dirt below, where the flea-beetles and the root-weevils awaited lovers' demise.

Ray had told Ahmad to reserve the best table in the house, number seven, the one right in front of the river-stone fireplace, where once a British film actor had proposed to an Ethiopian super-model with the cheeks of an Egyptian Sphinx and the grin of a Vatican Madonna. If all went right, *he* was planning to pop the question tonight over two crystal flutes of pink-champagne, down on one knee like he'd seen in that old Cary Grant movie.

Sure, he'd reasoned with himself, I've known Jenna less than a week, but you mustn't dilly-dally when you enter the flowered garden of true love! You inhale the jasmine-wishes and lavender-hopes like a bewitched bumblebee. And what you *never* do is hem-n-haw while your one true love is furtively glancing around the garden admiring the other wishing bees!

Jenna's *yes I will* would start his long-delayed journey toward seventh heaven, cloud nine, delivering him to the paradise that awaits all good men, those misunderstood creatures who have spent untold years laboring in the abject poverty of loneliness.

NINE

Marie had named the baby John Quincy Addams, after the sixth president of the United States, even though she knew the original John Quincy had spelled his last name with only one '*d*'. She still thought it was cute. When the baby's father, Gator Addams, finally showed up at the maternity ward in his usual drunken stupor the day after little Johnny was born, he told Marie he didn't give a shit *what* she named the bastard, she could call him *Nathaniel Fuckin' Hawthorne* for all he cared. Besides, he'd been telling his bar-buddies that he wasn't even sure the kid was *his*. Marie would "suck any half-hard cock that wiggled its scabby flea-bitten head at her!"

Johnny's childhood wasn't the best, to be sure. His dad left mama and him only eight months after he was born, disappearing into that yawning yaw that all 'disgusted with life' fathers flee to when the responsibilities of taking care of a family become a giant burden, a weight his misanthropic shoulders can't support. Marie had turned to crystal meth by that time to cope with the pathetic wretchedness of her *own* life. The dopamine highs were wonderful, but the come downs brought on hallucinations and delusions. *Twice* she tried to kill herself. Once deliberately overdosing on sleeping pills on Johnny's fourth birthday, medics showing up at the door of the shabby apartment being a great present for the kid. Once slitting her wrists in the bathtub on Valentine's Day, Marie sad and depressed because none of her scummy boyfriends had the common decency to even send her a card, a box of candy, *anything*, to show their thanks for various blow-jobs and butt fucks.

Needless to say, after the second attempt, the state put Johnny in a foster-home run by a mean child-beater and a serial pedophile. Of course *that* didn't end well! Johnny ran away when he was seven and was taken in by an older street-urchin named Adonis, who introduced the youngster to pickpocketing and purse-snatching. Tourists never saw them coming, the men usually back at the hotel before they missed their wallets, the women trying to pay for their chocolate éclairs and mocha Frappuccino's, then searching fruitlessly for their, by this time, three blocks away purses.

When he was nine, Johnny caught the eye of a sleazy producer of X-Rated movies, pandering to middle-aged men who liked to watch boys frolic around in their tighty-whities. Sleaze promised Johnny fifty dollars a day, but after four days of filming, he and video camera and two hundred dollars disappeared and that was the glorious end of Johnny's Hollywood career.

Well, blah-blah-blah, the same old story of a million other unwanted and thrown-away boys, abused and exploited and manipulated by a 'don't give a shit' society, and jump ahead twenty years to Johnny working at a Greek diner on Forty-Seventh washing dishes and sweeping floors. The Greek rented him a room above the diner for $375 a month, leaving Johnny only $300 to spend on toothpaste, deodorant, hair-gel and strip clubs. Obviously, the strip clubs got half of his funny-money, for what else does a cynical, pathetic loser spend his paycheck on but entrance to the illusory wonderland of tits and asses, lap dances and hand-jobs?

John Quincy could only afford *three* skank-wanks a month, the rest of the time he'd sit in the back rows wiggling himself, only occasionally being busted by some bad-tempered brute of a bouncer, then being told he was 86ed from the premises. And it was at one of those clubs he was still allowed in that some acne faced *pervert* tried to touch Johnny's pants-snake. A pen-knife in the thigh quickly halts any untoward trouser-feel, usually chasing the pervert out of the club, but on this occasion, Acne-Face ran and squealed to the bouncer who collared Johnny and phoned the city's finest. By that time Acne-Face had disappeared.

A stripper was engaged in a long $40 lap-dance one row away and witnessed the stab, showing up in court to corroborate the missing pervert's story, and John Quincy got one-to-three inside *without* his knife at the mercy of a *lot* of trouser-feelers. He vowed he'd never forget the face of that skank on the witness stand and promised himself that when he got out he'd make her pay.

TEN

It was beautiful outside and the lovers decided to walk the ten blocks to Michaelangelo's. The last vestiges of honey-evening's crimsoning light were blushing pink before the flirting gaze of lilac-veiled settling night. The sleepy leaves on the yawning elm trees were curving in their silken edges to prepare for another peaceful night's rest. As lovers passed the vacant lot between the Apollo Dry Cleaners and the tire store, male crickets lullabied their sexiest chirps in vainglorious attempts to mesmerize any nearby females into welcoming their romantic overtures. The baseball pennants hanging from the awning of Kramer's Betting Parlor danced with the wooing breeze. Even a stray swallowtail butterfly, looking lost and searching for its kaleidoscope of family and friends, seemed to be enjoying its first fluttering foray through the vespering city. The whole world was at peace.

As a full yellow moon rose over the horizon and caressed the timid cloud-maidens, Ray pulled Jenna closer to him, her head leaning on his shoulder as they strode beneath the first winking stars. Had the planet been created 4.5 billion years ago from the dust and gas of the solar nebula, then populated with 130 billion mammals, 400 billion birds, 3 trillion fish, 10 quintillion insects and 5 billion humans so that two lonely, lover-less people would find each other in the boundless, timeless universe? Was the astoundingly immeasurable past all meant to lead to this one moment where everything finally made sense, a moment all the celestial gears clicked into place? Was all of destiny designed to enable Ray and Jenna to unite in a glorious, spectacular, breathtaking celebration of true love? Ray liked to think so.

ELEVEN

The inmates hung around in groups of two to over a dozen men. On the cracked blacktop basketball court five Latinos and five African-Americans double-dribbled, elbowed, and trash-talked their way to an eventual ten-man pile-on, a fist and foot molly-whop. The weight-lifters counted their reps out by the iron pile, the gumps sneaking peeks at their biceps. The tattoos congregated by the barbed-wire fence mean-eyeballing the shaved heads. Here and there a pumpkin sat alone, avoiding unnecessary eye contact, especially with the J-cats and monkey-mouths. Most pumpkins just wanted to do their time with a minimum of trouble.

John Quincy Addams stayed in the wall-shadows reading a lop-eared paperback copy of Rip Van Winkle by Washington Irving, wishing *he* could sleep his way thru the next three years like that lucky Rip. Wake up when he'd served his time and then go his merry way. He'd only been here four days and the wolves were following him everywhere, there was one big ugly one leaning against the basketball pole leering at him now. John Quincy needed a road-dog to guard his back but he didn't know anybody that well yet, and he trusted *nobody*. Fresh meat was always on the grill with these guys.

A whistle blew ending recreation time and John Quincy herded in with the others. It was two hours to chow and instead of slow-footin' it to the TV room to watch reruns of Gomer Pyle, he plodded to his cell to get a little shut-eye. His bunkie was already there, going thru John's short stack of prison-library books. That irritated him but the guy was one of those fatty dump-trucks who considered other bunkies' belongings fair game, and besides, he had previously informed John, "I's jus' as soon *sit* on ya as talk ta ya, ya little runt!" John Quincy didn't need the aggravation.

TWELVE

Table seven was set with Christofle silverplated silverware. Michealangelo's owned only four five-piece settings and reserved them for the finest of customers. The last time they had been used was when the Princess of Denmark visited, well before Ahmad's *or* Ray's time. But the assistant manager wanted to do something special to thank Ray for filling in at the last minute for that scoundrel Anson. Ray had let on to Ahmad that he planned to ask Jenna to marry him and Ahmad promised to help make the proposal as wonderfully stunning as he could. Rene Ozorio indigo plates and Baccarat Massena crystal water goblets completed a table-setting fit for a princess. Add in a Waterford vase bearing a single Lincoln red rose and you had the makings of a romantic table Athena and Astarte would go to war over.

The lovers arrived at seven-thirty, after Jenna spent fifteen minutes beside the fountain teaching Ray just how she liked to be kissed: a soft snow-flake lip nuzzle turning into an avalanche of wanton tongue-searching that reached right into your angel's scarlet-tulip soul to quench the desolation of a thousand years of gloomy loneliness and moaning heartache. For a minute Ray lost all consciousness of romantic dinners and I-dos and just wanted to remain inside Jenna's soul exploring an emerald-laden universe stretching as far as a dream is wide.

The fireplace was burning with red-oaken logs harvested from the valley forest. Ahmad pulled out Jenna's cross-back velvet-cushioned chair, charmingly seating the most tantalizing creature Ahmad had ever seen or would see. Linen cloth-napkins found trembling laps, cabernet sauvignon cascaded into delicate long-stemmed glasses, smile waved to smile, and eyes never left eyes. The Maine lobster and pureed brussels sprouts barely lit their taste buds as the conversation floated on diaphanous wings between rainbow-sherbeted lovers, ruby-frosted words of enchanting futures and cherished plans accompanying pink sighs of happiness wrapped in summer-warmed cocoons.

Ray had fallen head-over-heels in love and Jenna was just beginning her fall.

THIRTEEN

"That punkin's ripe for a corin'," spat Earl. "We'll initiat' 'im ta'nite at th' showers," hissed Abner, "th' fish'll nev'r see it comin'."

Indeed, even though John Quincy was ever alert, always glancing over his shoulder in case some wolf cut a duck in for a deuce of joints to look the other way for twenty minutes, he *didn't* see it coming.

Friday nights Rowe was on shower-guard duty and he was as crooked as Red Riding Hood's path thru the woods to grandma's house. John Quincy was soaping up in stall four, only one other inmate in the shower room, in stall nine, when Abner, after passing Rowe a packet of meth, shoved John up against the tile and held him in a headlock as Earl corn-balled him. John fought back the best he could but Abner and Earl were both twice his size and three times as strong. Ten minutes later the mean, bad and ugly were gone, it was slam-bam-thank-you-mam. John picked himself up off the tile floor, stumbling and bumping off the wall, gasping for air thru his bruised windpipe. Leaning against the wall, ragged-gray water droplets continuing to bounce off his shaky legs, he knew he was now a full-fledged member of the bean-slot gang, his buttcrack a little roomier than yesterday.

He gingerly dried himself off, going a little slower and easier on his backside, then slipped into his blue peels and white bo-bos. *Well,* actually that wasn't *so* bad, he thought, now that *that* was out of the way, maybe the next 1,091 days would go smoother. Still, he'd need to find a reliable road-dog to watch his back in the shower from now on.

FOURTEEN

Richard set two generous slices of Italian cheesecake topped with Amaou strawberries in front of Ray and Jenna.

"*Bon appétit, jeunes amants!*" he wished.

Ray fumbled for the petite box inside his jacket pocket he'd been cherishingly guarding all night. As he pulled the black velvet ring-holder out, he clumsily dropped it to the floor and it rolled to rest against Jenna's left foot.

He's gonna *propose* to me! she thought. What kinda guy does that to a girl he just met? A *nice* one, that's who! She reached under the table to retrieve this precious ark of Ray's eternal *miraculous* love.

Miraculous because how often does an exotic dancer, a bump-and-grinder, a thong-cinnabon get a decent, kind, romantic man to actually care about her, care enough to make her his soul-mate for life, promise to love and protect her from a cruel, brutish, heart-wrenching world full of degenerate overcoat-jerkers and sadistic thigh-stabbers? Tomorrow's newspapers might feature the headline: '*Nice Guy Proposes to Lap-Dancer!*'

Jenna handed the box back to Ray as he pushed his chair aside and kneeled on one quivering knee.

"Jenna, I promise to love, cherish and treasure you for the rest of our lives. Keep you from harm, shield you from danger, and walk by your side thru every thunderstorm, every blizzard, every tempest, until the end of time! Will you marry me?"

Wow! thought Jenna, this is just like Billy Crystal proposing to Meg Ryan in *'Harry Met Sally'*.

Not really, this was better, much better. This wasn't a crowded Hollywood studio, these weren't actors. No one was there to say *"Cut! Let's try it again!"* They didn't have to. The scene was perfect. Thru her tears, Jenna exclaimed, *"Yes,* a thousand times *Yes!"* And so the *real* grand journey began.

FIFTEEN

The rice was streaming and the congratulations were scampering over the happy newly-weds' happy heads. The small group of well-wishers included only Cynane, Richard, Alexander and Ahmad with a very serious Richard serving as bestman.

"Now tie straight, cuff-links showing, white silk handkerchief at a 45 degree angle in your left breast-pocket," Richard had said.

Morty had wanted to come but Jenna told him to "go fly a kite!" She *still* hadn't told Ray she was a dancer. Morty'd be *sure* to spill the beans, make a sick joke, say something stupid like, "Baby-Dol', gu'ss this means th' end of m' be'jays," then that high squealing mockingbird laugh of his.

What's *wrong* with me? she thought, what kinda happy bride *lies* to her husband about where she works? A deceitful one, she sadly admitted to herself. But then what was to be gained from telling the guy who worshipped the ground you walked on that you were in fact *not* a fancy downtown paralegal but a girl-toy for perverts and misfits? Hm, maybe *she* was the misfit. She'd tell Ray, she promised herself, just not today, he looked too happy.

They all walked the six blocks from the city clerk's office to Michaelangelo's where a reception had been set up in the banquet room. A few round tables sat before a raised platform holding a six-foot linen-covered walnut trestle where the bride and groom were to be seated. Ahmad had given several of the busboys and one of the bartenders the afternoon off with pay so they could help fill out the room.

Champagne corks were popped, crystal flutes were raised and Richard proposed the toast.

"Here's to our finest up-and-coming young chef and his beautiful bride. May there always be a silver lining in every gray cloud and may they find pots of gold at the end of every rainbow!"

"Thank you, Richard," spoke a truly appreciative Ray, "nothing would make me happier than to continue working with such incredible and loving friends," "and colleagues," he added, noticing the antsy busboys at the back table who looked like they couldn't wait to get at the wedding-cake. "I know it's been a whirl-wind romance but let me assure all you kind folks that, to paraphrase a supreme court justice, I know love when I see it!"

There was laughter and applause then Cynane tapped a spoon against her champagne glass and said, "Here, here, time for the beautiful bride's speech."

Jenna arose, her off-white wedding veil barely hiding the tears of joy. In a voice not bad for a lap-dancer, she sang lyrics she said she recently wrote to a Noel Paul Stookey tune:

Ray, I'll nourish you, honor and respect you,
help you feel better when you're feeling blue,
        but, Dear, I gotta be me,
            independent and free,
                and not a mere reflection of you;

I'll stand close beside you whenever you need me,
comfort and console you if ever you should weep,
        but, Dear, I hafta believe
            anything I achieve
                is not a mere reflection of you;

I will clutch you tight when you're sad and lonesome,
raise you up whenever you're discouraged and glum,
        but assure me you'll agree
            I can have my own dreams
                and be not a mere reflection of you.

The small gathering was at first stunned. You could hear a pin drop, then Ahmad started clapping and the busboys *huzzah-ed!* If Ray coulda smiled any wider we'd have a new *Grand Canyon.*

SIXTEEN

Billy was a precocious kid, always following his big brother Ray around pointing out things that Ray had never even contemplated, like bees never sleep, or the sky isn't really blue, it only *looked* blue because of the way the sun's light is reflected. Who cared? thought Ray, he had other things to worry about, like when are the Yankees gonna start winning games again. Still, he loved the little pest, despite his irrelevant facts about nature; but leave those earth-shattering discoveries to the science guys who care about such useless drivel!

But Billy always bragged to Ray he was gonna grow up and *become* one of those science-guys, discover a new unified theory of relativity, or a way to create a cold-fusion machine. His school grades didn't agree, though. His teachers said he was lazy, that he was one of those kids who dreamily stared out the classroom window watching the clouds float by while they were trying to *teach* the students something.

By the time Billy reached high school, all hopes of getting into college were squelched by *C's* and *D's*. Even a good trade-school was out of the question; how do you teach a kid to tune a car or fix a washing machine when he was constantly wondering about bee-sleep and blue skies?

Ah, but there's one miraculous answer to save these dreamers, these cloud-gazers, one ripple-glorious career that can make real valued *citizens* out of them, people that society respects and honors and rewards: the Military. They could train the most day-dreamiest cloud-watcher how to forget all about tawny-theories, crimson-concepts, silver-speculations. Fiddle-de-dee to all that *druck;* see the world, fight the bad guys, save humanity from everything un-American, all that foreign *garbage-talk* of non-intervention in others' affairs that unceasingly pollutes the fine and noble ideas of capitalism and free enterprise. Let the laissez-faire sin-prophets who fund the Pentagon show its soldiers what a *real* world should look like.

So Billy enlisted. What choice did he have? What *other* ruby-shimmering existences awaited him? Three squares and a bed would give him time to reassess his future, repaint and remodel his fading dreams.

Except this new world of drill-sergeants and KP duty didn't leave Billy much time to ponder futures and dreams. He did have *one* exceptional talent, though: out on the firing range he could 'knock a penny off a canteen' at two hundred yards. His sergeant awarded him lead marksman of company E. Okay big deal, Billy thought, where's *that* gonna get him? Some assignment sniping Iraqis off crumbling buildings? That was the *last* thing he wanted, let the war-machine find another cog. So he started *missing* the 'penny', and soon enough, he was assigned to new digs, the base kitchen, learning the art of fine army cuisine under the tutelage of one Moses C. Christopher.

Moses always told soldiers that the C stood for *chef,* but it really stood for Cletis, his dad wanting to name him after Clete Boyer, the long-time Yankee third-baseman. His mom won out, though, Moses standing for *her* favorite hero, Moses from the Good Book. Good call, too. Her son became a miracle-worker in the kitchen!

In Ray's most recent letter to Billy, he told him he was working as a cook at a fancy steakhouse called Michaelangelo's. Good, Billy had written back, maybe when his time was up Big Brother could get him a job there.

SEVENTEEN

Moses Cletis Christopher came out of Missouri. He grew up cheering for the K.C. Athletics, his dad Albert's favorite team. The A's were usually the worst team in the American League, basically a farm-team for the New York Yankees. Among other good young players the A's *gifted* to N.Y. was the homer-hitting Roger Maris, who shortly thereafter broke Babe Ruth's thirty-four year old homerun record. But the trade that broke Albert's heart was when the A's sent phenom Cletis Boyer to the Yankees.

'Clete' was a slick-fielding third-baseman who played in five consecutive World Series for N.Y. He grew up in Alba, Missouri, Albert's home town. As a matter of fact, Albert worked with Clete's father, Vern, at the marble factory. When Clete was traded, Albert vowed he was 'done' with the A's, and actually *cheered* when the team moved to Oakland. *Good Riddance! Who Needs Ya!* Within four years the A's were in the World Series. One city's junk is another city's fortune. Albert and Moses became die-hard Yankee fans, that is until N.Y.

traded Clete to Atlanta. But by that time, Moses was at Fort Riley, Kansas.

At nineteen, Moses had been drafted. Vietnam was beginning to rage and he wanted no part of the fighting, so he volunteered for the cooks' program, learning all the intricacies of pepper pot soup and turkey loaf. He was assigned to Fort Riley, Kansas, less than 300 miles from home, cooking for some of the first soldiers to deploy to Southeast Asia. He was thankful he wasn't among them. Moses decided to become a 'lifer', eventually crossing paths with Billy, who wasn't from Missouri and had never heard of Clete Boyer, had never thought of how a team can tear a fan's heart out, stomp it into dream-dust, and laugh all the way to a place called Oakland.

A place called Oakland, where many of Fort Riley's soldiers were sent before being moved to Vietnam, as the Military Industrial Complex stomped *their* hearts into dream-dust and laughed all the way to record profits.

EIGHTEEN

The Latinos and African-Americans were double-dribbling and trash-talking again. Another molly-whopper wasn't far off. John Quincy Addams was huddling in the morning shade of the South Wall talking to a spider-monkey doing hard-time on a liquor store bust-up gone wrong. Spider was only trying to get $300 to buy a new dress for his girl and a pair of used Michael Jordans for him when some stupid middle-aged suburban *hero* walked in, realized he was interrupting a crime scene, and like Dirty Harry, pulled his Magnum and yelled, "go ahead, punk, make my day!" The *punk* spun around and in a split second, Dirty Harry was lying on the tile floor, a .32 in his liver. What made these guys think a two-hour class on shooting and a permit made them the answer to everything that was wrong with the world?

Spider-Monkey hit the parking-lot empty-handed, sprinted down a side street, turned a corner, and ran right into a cop car, the officer enjoying his morning Crispy Crème and coffee. Spider bounced off the car door and the gun flew right thru the open window landing on the officer's surprised lap. Sometimes a punk's luck just runs out!

John Quincy and Spider-Monkey had something in common: they'd been taking care of business, just looking for a quick score, John an overcoat orgasm, Spider a pair of sneakers, when *fate,* that great even-upperer of good deeds and bad deeds, crossed both their paths.

From that first day they met, they felt fate was trying to make it up to them by making them road-dogs, protectors of each other's backs, musketeers pledging 'one for all, all for one', taking on every and all attackers together, defending one another to the death. No more surprise shower-shoves, no suffering a Duck's grinning deceitful obliviousness, no falling helpless victim to wolves, dump-trucks or any other 'evils of the night'. They both spit in their palms, shook hands, and road-dogs it was!

NINETEEN

The honeymoon cabin was perched on the edge of the Columbia River Gorge overlooking Lake Gillette. From the bedroom window the lake sparkled like teardrop-shaped diamonds, though there were no tears in *this* bedroom. Ray had spent the previous night in the Land of Ecstasy, a place where only the luckiest of lovers, the most blessed of star-struck husbands, are ever allowed to enter, and *only* if escorted by a Princess of Paradise, a Royal Shepherdess of the Elysian Fields of Rhapsody, nay a *Queen* of Valhalla. Jenna appeared to Ray as *all* of these things.

She steered him thru sapphire valleys of quivering jubilance, transported him over trembling mountains of euphoria, squired him past vibrating plains of intoxication. No muscle was left unused, no tendon ignored, no joint neglected.

The bride performed like an Olympic gymnast determined to win every gold medal in the World's Preeminent Lover category: 180-degree splits, full-twisting back tucks, backward straddle-jumps, segueing into a double-pike dismount, leaving the groom delirious and babbling on about burnt sweet potato souffles and scorched vanilla crème brûlées. Ray soon did his own segue from blinking, feverish, whirling dervish into a deep, peaceful sleep, the calmest, most tranquil night's rest he'd ever had.

The Lake Gillette sparkling diamonds danced in shimmering little reminders of honeymooners' precious rewards.

Honeymoon at an end, Ray and Jenna returned to the city. The lovers found a two-bedroom flat in the Village and moved in together. Jenna quit Morty's, signed up for a para-legal course at the junior college, assuring Ray she was pursuing an advanced degree, kind of a lie, but eliminating the need to ever confess to her new, trusting, adoring husband about her not so enchanting work-past.

Anson was back cheffing the dinner shift, Ray back handling the lunch crowd, routines resumed.

Almost a year passed, life was good. Until it wasn't.

Part Two

TWENTY

"The purpose of this hearing is to determine your suitability for release. Have you prepared a statement for this board?"

"Yes, sir, I have," spoke John Quincy in a firm yet respectful voice, trying to sound confident yet deferential, like an impala cornered by a tiger, who assures the cat, "I realize it's your dinner time, but if you let me go take care of some business, I promise to show up here again tomorrow morning at ten."

John Quincy stated, "I am sorry for what I did, I made a mistake that I've regretted ever since. I'm a changed man."

"And how have you changed?"

"I've learned violence is never the answer. Communication is always the best solution to any misunderstanding."

The parole hearing examiner adjusted his taped-up Bausch and Lomb tortoiseshells, asking, "And what are your future plans?"

"I want to lead a law-abiding life and become an upstanding citizen of society," lied John Quincy, thinking to himself, yeah, as upstanding as a bull in a china shop.

"You will be notified of the commission's decision within 21 business days. You may return to your cell."

I'd like to get *your* ass inside my cell for ten minutes, you *wonk!* fantasized John Quincy.

But twenty-one business days later, he walked thru the prison gate a free man. Well, not really *free!* He'd been assigned to a halfway house on MacDougal Street at the edge of the Village. The parole release letter said he had twenty-four hours to report to his case manager. He was gonna miss Spider, he mused, but he'd stay in touch. They were road-dogs, after all, musketeers, fate-mates, side-kicks, spit-buds.

What does a free man do with 24 hours? mused John Quincy, what else, titty-bar, here I come!

TWENTY-ONE

Popeye Williams was an ex-bodybuilder, nicknamed after the cartoon character because of his bulging forearm muscles and his penchant for pipe-smoking. It didn't hurt that his girlfriend's name was Olive. Go figure.

When Popeye was twenty-four, he'd finished third in the citywide Middleweight Amateurs Contest. His coach urged him to go pro and Popeye trained hard for eight months. Then a bench-press barbell slipped and broke his collar-bone. After the long lay-off, he could not quite get back to peak performance and decided to retire from the sport. He kept working out with lighter weights to stay in shape and good thing! Two years later he met the fourth-place Miss New England Under 25 fitness model, Olive O., and a nickname was born.

Popeye was working as a fitness instructor at Gatt's Gym, but old man Gatt had been thru The Depression and watched every penny. His employees called him 'chintzy as a cat who's cornered a whole family of mice and won't share them with his alley-buddies'.

Olive's brother made pretty decent money working as a parole officer and told Popeye that because of the recent explosion in prison populations, the state had suspended requirements that officers needed college degrees. This seemed a golden opportunity for Popeye and he jumped on it. After three months training, he was assigned to a halfway house on MacDougal Street.

TWENTY-TWO

"The secret to perfect scrambled eggs is milk, eight tablespoons per dozen eggs," instructed Moses C. Christopher. "The manual says use water, but that's bullshit. The problem is gettin' that chintzy Commander to buy 'nough milk. I also mix in a tablespoon of lemon juice and a teaspoon of starch for each egg. Commander won't requisition me olive oil, *my* personal favorite, so I plop a big dollop of butter into the skillet. I don't add no onions or cheese, many of the grunts don't like 'em that way. Let 'em sprinkle on their own salt and pepper. Now here's the key, Billy, turn off the burner just before they're done cookin' but keep stirrin'. You'll get the hang of it, kid, it'll take a while, but what else ya got? I'll make a chef outta ya yet!"

Moses was right, what else *does* a military guy got but time? In one way a military stretch is like a prison stretch, both Billy and John Quincy had to pay the price for their decisions: Billy, a decision to serve his country, John Quincy, a decision to serve his vanity. Yet maybe enlisting and stabbing a pervert are *both* vanity moves, somehow making yourself feel like you're in control of your life when, really, consequences control *you*.

Anyway, Billy was glad to be in the kitchen with Moses. He had no appetite for doing an army's dirty work: killing so-called enemy soldiers who were only serving their *own* country. And America was always at war *somewhere!* Scrambling eggs and stroganoffing hamburger and creaming chipped-beef-on-toast could be a lot more soul-satisfying than patrolling the Iraqi desert or the Bosnian highlands or body-guarding some oil company in Africa.

And who knows, maybe a decent-paying job would come out of it. You listening Brother Ray?

TWENTY-THREE

But Brother Ray wasn't listening to Billy's secret hopes and wishes. What he *was* listening to was the sound of Lexi's high heels clickity-clacking across the tile kitchen floor. Ahmad had been promoted to full-time manager and Lexi, fresh out of restaurant-managing school, was the new assistant manager. Every time Ray heard those high heels clickity-clacking toward him, the front of his pants got a little tighter.

Michaelangelo's had been doing more lunch business than ever and Ray's cooking was mostly to thank. The owner was smiling like a hog in a pea-patch, and had rewarded Ray with a raise. The Mayor had *twice* sent his regards to the kitchen and had *raved* over the potatoes au gratin, now made exclusively with Netherlands gouda cheese.

The raise was fine and all, but the best thing that the owner ever did was hire Lexi, at least according to Ray's pants. Long blond hair, bright blue eyes and legs... ah those legs, dreamed Ray, how can you not drool like a fool over luscious legs like her's? What I wouldn't give to slowly remove those nylon stockings and bury my face in... *hold up,* drool-fool, he scolded himself, I'm married to the sexiest, most beautiful girl in the world. I should be ashamed of myself. *Still...*

"Sugar," drawled Lexi, "can you do me an itsy-bitsy favor and save me the T-bone steak leftovers for my poodle-dog, Aletta, *appreeeeeciate* it, Darlin'!"

I'd like to T-bone *her!* fantasized Ray. Stop it right *now,* you *reprobate,* Ray reprimanded himself, I got *Jenna* waiting at home!

TWENTY-FOUR

Thing was, Jenna *wasn't* waiting at home. She was now six months into her para-legal studies and had fallen all googly-eyes for her professor, Judge *Slick*. Slick because just about *every* female student fell googly-eyes for him, a few of the males, too, and Slick wasn't one to waste a crush, male *or* female. And right now, Jenna was the latest in the rotation.

Judge Summer, nee Slick, was the most distinguished-looking man Jenna had ever laid eyes on. And that *beard,* she sighed, she just wanted to take off her shoes and shrink herself and run nilly-willy all thru his luxurious, furry man-mane, let the thick curly hairs tickle her toes and fondle her ankles.

She sat in his classroom while he taught the students legalistic terms and how to draft legal correspondence. But the words wafted right over Jenna's infatuated head. She was spellbound by his caressing gaze, like a parakeet mesmerized by the rattlesnake's flicker-flamed, moonbeam-dazzled eyes, hypnotized by its *you-belong-to-me-now* stare, a parakeet ready to surrender its helpless innocence to the dangerous lullaby about to devour it.

The judge spoke about corporate law-suits, but Jenna was idol-oblivious to his precedents. He discussed inheritance law, but she was clueless to why she should care about such things if she could but only lay in his destiny-perfumed arms, gently butterfly-kiss his rapture-poemed lips, breathlessly ravish his star-god's body.

Oh, she was an *evil bad thing,* she thought to herself, so evil, she didn't even know how to describe herself, just a *thing,* bent on forgetting the one decent ingredient in her new life: Ray. Out of this whole indifferent, egotistical, soulless world, *Ray* had shown up on her lonely doorstep, flowers in hand, *flowers,* offering a genuine, unfeigned smile, unlike those lascivious ogre-grins that the *perverts* at Morty's petrified her heart with. *Still...*

TWENTY-FIVE

As often happens in the affairs of men and women, a happy wife finds herself in the arms of a lover who's *not* her husband. One moment she is fantasizing about a guy's beard, the next moment she's in his bed.

The Judge had no qualms about bedding a student who was happily married. What *was* happiness, anyway? The philosophers and poets have debated this conundrum for centuries, never really coming up with a satisfactory definition.

Was it contentment, prosperity, good-health, abundance of good-luck, hope for the future? Jenna had all these, and more. When she was in *Ray's* arms, she felt content. They had their own apartment and a savings account, *that* felt prosperous. She had her health, felt lucky finding a good man, and had hopes for a successful and rewarding future.

And yet, here she *was,* lying naked next to Judge Summers, running her fingers thru his thick dark chest hairs, her searching nostrils smelling his Jack Daniel's-scented beard, her lips tasting his wet, probing caramel-and-cinnamon-flavored tongue.

She felt as if she'd been sucked thru a heaving interstellar wormhole, hurtling from one dimension to another, from one *time* to another, whirling and careening off blazing-hot planets, barreling and coursing thru untold galaxies, desperately crying out: *take me, take me, take me!*

The Judge took her. Took her with all the force of a swirling scarlet cloud of unbearably-hot solar-plasma, his neon aurora enveloping her in buffeting, lurching, frothing everythingness, a spiraling, churning maelstrom of blistering, explosive power. Jenna blacked out, one thought repeating itself over and over in her trembling mind: *Ray must never know, Ray must never know…*

TWENTY-SIX

"No drugs, no alcohol, no pets, no fighting, no stealing, and *no women!* You can have dirty magazines and cigarettes. Curfew's at 9pm, phone calls are limited to fifteen minutes twice a day. You gotta get fulltime employment, I'll help you with that. Violate *any* rule and I'll have you back in stir so fast that head'll spin! Got it?"

"Yeah," grunted John Quincy.

"That's yes sir," corrected Popeye, "when you address me."

"Yeah *sir!*" John Quincy grunted a little louder, thinking, *my* rule would have you suckin' my dick, you muscle-bound queer!

"Chores include one hour of kitchen duty a day and two hours of general cleaning. Vacuums, mops and cleaning supplies are in the janitor's closet, don't even *think* of sniffin' the *Mr. Clean!* If you're a good boy and don't get into trouble, I'll have you outta here in six months. It's up to you, *got it?*" asked Popeye.

Yak, yak, yak, blubber, blubber, blubber, said John Quincy to himself, why don't you go and work on that left arm, *mutant,* it's a little smaller than the right one. But out loud he lipped, "Got it." Boy, I'd like to take a pin and *pop* those muscles, the carnival freak, he'd probably *swoosh* into the sky like a punctured balloon!

So MacDougal Street was John Quincy's new digs and Popeye his stay-out-of-jail card!

TWENTY-SEVEN

Now that Ahmad was Michaelangelo's manager, he did all the hiring and firing. On this particular dreary, overcast Saturday morning he had two job interviews scheduled. One was with the kid brother of his star lunch-chef, the other was with some ex-con a high-school-buddy-turned-parole-officer was sending over. Ahmad was all for giving ex-cons a break, but the only things he trusted them with were dirty dishes and mops.

Smack dab at nine o'clock, Billy knocked on Ahmad's half-open office door.

"C'mon in, kiddo, Ray's told me a lot about ya, ready ta go ta work? We don't need ta go thru the formality of an application or background check, Ray's word is good enough for me! He says ya learned ta cook in the military. We do things different here, and yu'll find the food is miles ahead of Uncle Sam's, but yu'll be on track before ya know it. And Ray promised me he'd take ya under his wing. What else are big brothers for, right kiddo?"

Almost before Billy could nod thank-you, Ahmad yelled out for Lexi to show him the kitchen. She clickety-clacked in and Billy saw immediately what Ray had meant in his letters when he wrote: 'she's got legs that stretch from Mars to Jupiter', and when Billy heard her drawl, "Folla meeee, Cutie," understood now when Ray wrote: 'just her juicy twang alone will give you a hard-on six ways to Sunday!' She *was* juicy, Billy agreed.

At ten o'clock Ahmad's mood was a little more somber. John Quincy was sitting across from him and Ahmad thought, there's somethin' about this guy that just isn't right. He couldn't put his finger on it but he owed his parole-officer-buddy a favor for hooking him up with that Iranian car mechanic who repaired the steering on his '78 Mercedes after four other mechanics couldn't do it.

"Ever worked in a restaurant before?" asked the manager.

"Nope," was all John Quincy said.

This interview was gonna be a real thrill, mused Ahmad, what do they do in prison, teach these guys to use one-syllable words?

In his defense, John Quincy couldn't care less about restaurant jobs, *hell,* he thought, he didn't give a rat's ass about *any* job, it was that *dick* parole officer who grunted, "No job, no parole!" He'd take some pissy ant job but he'd be damned if he'd like it.

"All I got is the four ta midnight shift open," said Ahmad.

"Whatever," spat out John Quincy.

"Yu'll be washin' dishes and moppin' floors." Great! mumbled the ex-con under his breath, touchin' rich pricks' spit an' moppin' up shit.

"What's that now?" asked Ahmad.

"Nothin'!" hissed John Quincy.

Wow, thought Ahmad, as if I don't have *enough* to do, now every day I gotta count dishes and silverware.

TWENTY-EIGHT

Where *is* she? wondered Ray, who'd been calling Jenna at home off and on for two hours. She's got no class today, this is *Thanksgiving!* We went to D'agostino's Grocery yesterday to get the turkey and everything, and even if she forgot something, the Dag is closed today. It's just not like her to go somewhere without telling me! But before he could start worrying *too* much, Billy needed help with the potato gnocchi.

"How long do these taters cook?" asked Billy.

"Add a handful of salt and steam 33 minutes," hurriedly answered Ray, busy with his own fettuccine alfredo.

"My handful or yours?" replied Billy.

"Yours!" yelled Ray, who was starting to think maybe hiring his brother hadn't been his most brilliant idea.

"Don't yell at me, Ray, they don't have these fancy-smantzies on base."

Okay, Ray shook his head, okay, gotta show a little more patience with little brother. "You'll know when they're done when you can pierce 'em with a steak knife," he now said calmly, "then take 'em off the heat and mash 'em, just not by hand, they come out too gummy. Run 'em thru the potato ricer, just *once* mind you, sprinkle with flour and knead into a ball."

"What the hell's a potato ricer, Ray?"

"Over there next to the salad counter, by the blender."

Hm, teaching bro the tricks of the restaurant trade ain't gonna be easy, Ray saw, as he added garlic salt to his alfredo.

"Form ½ inch cylinders about a foot long then cut into ¾ inch cubes, boil those two minutes 'til they float, drain and add parmesan. Presto, you're done!"

I'll *never* be done learning how a rich man eats, reflected Billy.

It was two *more* hours and a lunch rush before Ray could try calling Jenna again. There was no answer, of course, she was just waking up from her trip through the wormhole.

TWENTY-NINE

Jenna emerged from the wormhole to a haze of tobacco smoke. Coughing, she turned over in bed to see the Judge sitting in a robe by a closed window.

"Can you open that window? I can hardly breathe!" hoarsely whispered Jenna.

The Judge raised it a crack, saying, "I hope my pipe isn't bothering you, dear."

At least that's what Jenna *hoped* he'd say. Instead he just grunted.

"What time is it?" asked Jenna.

"Time for all little para-legals to catch the subway home," muttered the Judge, "I'm going to my parents at three."

Jenna climbed out of bed and padded over to the window-seat and nestled into his warm lap like a turtle seeking a safe place to spend the winter. She burrowed her nose into the Judge's beard, still smelling of whiskey and paradise, kissing his neck and at the same time reaching to untie his robe, seeking that wondrous spaceship that had *thrusted* her quivering pink soul thru untold rhapsody-rippled galaxies.

The Judge pushed her hand away, saying roughly, "No time for *that*, you get dressed and get going."

He literally *pushed* her off his lap, Jenna now awkwardly sprawled on the carpet, her bare legs pointing up in the air like she was ready to be entered, but her shocked face revealing she had realized sex right now was probably a long shot. She nakedly stared up at the glaring Judge like a scraggly, scrawny mouse rejected and pawed aside by an unsatisfied alley cat looking for a more scrumptious dinner.

As the mocking sunlight poured in thru the window deluging her drowning desire, Jenna lowered her legs *and* any optimism of the anxious astronaut hoping to re-enter the wormhole leading to the far side of the universe where the welcoming god of ethereal expectations and diaphanous dreams awaited.

Letting the Judge fiddle in the bathroom, Jenna hurriedly threw on her skirt and sweater, still lying crumpled by the fireplace where he had undressed her. Apparently, wormholes just suck you in and after madly crashing your throbbing existence from one end of the cosmos to the other, showing you exhilarating, pulsating, sensual possibilities you never knew were imaginable, they deposit you right back where you began, back to that mortal singularity called reality.

THIRTY

Reality was where John Quincy was right now, sweating in front of an industrial dishwasher, scraping leftovers off rich people's china. The fat snots leave more leftovers on a plate than what I eat in a goddamned week, he babbled to himself.

He'd met Ray, said hello to Billy, nodded once or twice to Richard and Alexander, even played a little back-alley craps with the busboys, but that *slut* of an assistant manager hadn't given him the time of day. All she did was clickity-clack into the kitchen smiling at Ray and flirting with Billy, with that *drawl* he'd like to record and play back while he was whacking off to his magazines.

Oh, if only women were completely subservient to men, like those wives in Japan he'd been reading about. Japanese men *knew* how to treat *their* women, the dishwasher gloated! Marry them when they're thirteen, train 'em to be submissive, forbid them to speak unless spoken to, give them *all* the cooking and housekeeping duties, *fuck* all that American equality of the sexes bullshit!

If *he* was President, he'd pass a law making women virtual *slaves* to men, legalize rape, make every pussy free and available to any man who wants it, yeah, that's *my* kinda world, John Quincy fantasized, my kinda *paradise.* Then girls like Lexi would be clickity-clacking over to *me,* giving me anything I want any time I want it! No more paying for hand-jobs. Ahh, whatta world, he sighed, and closed his eyes dreaming. Hot water burning his hand brought him back to reality.

Reality was where Billy was right now, too. It seemed Lexi was constantly making trips to the kitchen on the pretense of asking Billy where the extra salt shakers were, or if he knew where she could find some candles. *Candles?* He was working the salad and dessert bar, what did he know about candles? If he didn't know better, he thought, the girl had the hots for him. Maybe he should ask her to stick around after closing time and have a beer with him, chat her up a bit, never know, he might have a chance.

John Quincy watched Lexi flirt and bat her eyelashes at Billy, it made him *sick.* Girls like that were good for one thing only: lickin' dicks. He flicked out his tongue and grabbed his crotch. Well, if they were gonna do it, at least they could let him watch!

Ray looked over and saw the new dishwasher leering at his brother, wondering what this guy had against Billy. Better keep his eye on this weirdo, he thought, dishwashers were a dime a dozen, prisons were full of them.

But dolls like Lexi *weren't* a dime a dozen. Billy had been with beautiful girls before, but there was beautiful and there was *drop dead gorgeous!* If I got even an ice cube's chance in hell to bed her, he told himself, I ain't gonna waste it just smiling and winking. I'm gonna drop myself into that ninety-dollar *bourbon* before I melt!

THIRTY-ONE

That evening when Ray opened the apartment door, the smell of roasting turkey and pumpkin pie smiled at him. He walked into the kitchen and kissed his wife.

"Where *were* you? I called and called!"

"Oh, I subwayed over to get some cheddar cheese at Murray's," Jenna lied, "I know how you like it on your broccoli."

She felt terrible. This was the first lie she had ever told Ray. Okay, not true, she remembered, there was the erotic dancer ruse, but that was more of an *avoidance*.

"Why didn't you just call me? I coulda brought some home from the restaurant." Ray asked.

"Wow, I never thought of that!" The lie kept getting longer and longer like a string unreeling a kite into the windy sky where it soon becomes just a speck of bright paper, a speck of truth. What am I supposed to tell him? Jenna asked herself, I was having unbelievable tantric sex all morning with my professor?

After Ray showered, they sat down to dinner, the first Thanksgiving they had ever spent alone. But the turkey was under-cooked and there was American cheese on the broccoli. Ray said nothing. Preparing a Thanksgiving dinner was a humongous job, getting cheddar and American mixed up seemed a minor detail. He let it go. He would have preferred to make the dinner himself, after all he *was* a professional cook, but Jenna insisted on doing the home-cooking herself, bless her heart, even though she wasn't very good at it. But he'd never tell, her delicious *bedroom* recipes made up for it.

Following the burnt pumpkin pie, they tupperwared the leftovers and did the dishes. After folding the drying towel on the oven handle, Ray stared in utter amazement at his achingly beautiful wife, her caressing eyes, her candied lips, her coy nose, her captivating hair, all his.

"*What?*" *Jenna* whispered.

"It's just *you,* your beauty, it takes my breath away!"

In that moment Jenna wished she'd never heard of the Judge, never let his snake-eyes hypnotize her, never let his snake-hiss call her into his lair, his nest, his bed! *Here* was all she needed, all she had ever wished for, *her* miracle, *her* godsend! For if there was truly a god in heaven, then *He* had sent her this man, this blessing, this *wonder,* to save her from the crushing desolation of helplessness, the callous illusion of obliviousness, all the ugly, harmful pain of a horrible existence without love.

This is where she wanted to be, *needed* to be, today, tomorrow, forever! Holding his hand, she led her husband to the bedroom, into the oven of carnal delights, cherry pies and apricot muffins, raspberry meringue and peach pudding. Ray got his delicious bedroom recipes!

Afterward, laying in each other's arms, they watched the re-run of The Flintstone Thanksgiving Special, both laughing when Dino locked Fred out of the house and he yelled "*Wilmaaaa!*"

THIRTY-TWO

Wilma had *nothing* on Lexi. The pretty girls Billy had been with had always been a disappointment. They all looked like a million dollars and made love like a counterfeit twenty. But Lexi? That girl screwed like a *billion* dollars, Billy smiled. And smiled. And smiled. And smiled. It might have been the best sex he ever had, pretty girl *or* ugly girl.

Maybe ice cubes really *do* have a chance in hell. After work Billy had invited Lexi to stick around and have that beer. To his pleasant surprise, she agreed. Beer turned to rum, smile turned to wink, and a dance turned to "my place or yours?" Billy's bed was the big winner. And when they were done, Lexi didn't slip on her panties and make some excuse for leaving, "I got an early morning" or "I gotta get home to feed the dog", no, she stayed the night. In the morning she showed Billy a few more dollars, then made him pancakes and coffee. He was in love!

But what does an assistant cook barely making more than minimum wage have to offer a girl of Lexi's looks and talents besides his own talented cock? Billy smirked. She'd sure as molasses end up with one of those rich pricks always waltzing into Michaelangelo's throwing their probably ill-gotten hundred-dollar bills around. I hate this world, he said to himself, it's the undeserving bastards who always win.

After showering with Billy and giving him the best handjob he'd had since fourteen-year-old Betty Lou jerked him on the Coney Island Ferris wheel during their high school field trip, Lexi clickity-clacked home for a quick change of clothes and a metro ride to the restaurant, saying she'd see him there later, and that it was understandable if he showed up a little late for work, he'd *earned* the privilege. She'd clear it with Ahmad with a little sweet talk.

Okay, Billy assured himself, I'll ride this thing as long as Jesus permits, ride it as long as the law allows. He did have his *own* bedroom talents going for him. But when one of those rich pricks turned her pretty head? Jesus couldn't save him then.

THIRTY-THREE

Jesus couldn't save Jenna either. She had told herself she'd never cheat on Ray again. But secret promises like that evaporate like morning dew off a sunlit daffodil. When the snake tells the parakeet *you belong to me now,* the little bird is indeed helpless, lost in the new reality of the snake controlling its destiny.

Each day in school, Jenna would fall oblivious to everything around her, the ticking clock on the wall, students whispering the latest college gossip, even the buzzing bell signaling end of class. As her comrades filed out, she'd continue to stare at her snake, ready to dreamily tweet *Master, command me!*

But the snake had lost interest, there was a new parakeet in the love-jungle, Dawn, the one with the big green eyes, eyes saying, *I'm ready to be eaten!*

Jenna would smooth her ruffled feathers and miserably hop-hop out the door, past the rival green-eyed bird eagerly inching closer to her demise, Jenna's own sad eyes beseeching, pleading, *praying* that the Judge would smile at her, nod at her, glare at her, *anything.* One *Hello, Jenna* could re-assure her that the world *wasn't* an indifferent, impassive, insensitive place, but one still of empathy, gentleness and comfort.

He doesn't really know the tender, inner me, she ached, who I am, what I am, what I want him to see, *need* him to see. I just want a *glance,* even the mere *promise* of a glance, to prove to him I'm worth trusting, worth loving!

Jenna, this is Houston, do you read me? Have you forgotten about Ray again, that wonderful guy who married you, saved you from a career of dancing on perverts' laps? The guy who worships the ground you walk on, who thinks you're the most beautiful girl in the world, *his* world of gentleness and comfort?

As she continued to hop-hop out the classroom door, Jenna answered Houston. I'm coming home, she said.

THIRTY-FOUR

In *Wizard of Oz,* Dorothy said, "Home is where the love is!" Or something to that effect. That night when Ray opened the apartment door, Jenna was right inside waiting, naked, water droplets from her just finished shower still clinging for dear life to her Ivory-soap-smelling body, droplets *and* wife waiting to show one lucky husband what being sucked thru a wormhole felt like: the explosive, blistering, barreling from one galaxy to the next, the leaving of one moan-rippled dimension for another, the abandoning of all previously confirmed rules of time and space for an infinitely timeless, breathless, unimaginably exotic rendezvous with fate. This time it was Ray who blacked out, and Jenna the unbearably-hot solar-plasma, the churning maelstrom of *everythingness.*

Jenna had made a solemn vow that the Judge was history, a detour off Jenna-Ray Boulevard she never should have taken. From now on it was Ray, and only Ray, that she'd journey down life's highway with. They say all roads lead to paradise. But some roads are best avoided.

In the early morning darkness, Jenna awoke to the sound of Ray snoring. *Snoring?* Ray had never snored before, was that the slumber-melody of the guiltless, the blameless, the faultless, the stainless? Did *she* ever snore? Ray had never complained. But then, of course he wouldn't. He was too thoughtful, too loving, too *nice*. She'd often heard someone say, 'You're too nice!', meaning people were going to take advantage of you, run all over you, trample you *and* your good nature. Better to be leery, wary, suspicious of others' intentions, judgmental of every action of every*body*, no matter *how* loving and thoughtful.

Jenna shook her head, Ray didn't have a judgmental bone in his body. If *he* was too nice, then she needed *that* recipe, the whole world needed that recipe. She smiled at Ray resting so peacefully, so tranquilly, like he was dreaming of lollipops and rainbows, moonbeams and shooting stars. She gently brushed the hair away from his untroubled face, away from his *nice* face, and wondered: did Ray ever think bad of *anyone?*

Maybe he should've.

THIRTY-FIVE

John Quincy had a criminal record, and the State forbid those with criminal convictions from owning guns. That didn't stop John Quincy, he knew a *guy*. But he needed $300, and he needed a place to stash the weapon. Both problems had been solved when Michaelangelo's hired him. It took him a while to squirrel away the cash, but now he had it. He'd also discovered a place to hide it, an electronic rat-trap behind the milk-crates in the walk-in.

What cook or busboy would ever stick his hand in a rat-trap? John Quincy just had to not forget to check the trap occasionally to make sure no trapped rodent was inside gnawing on the pistol-handle. Those damn pests would eat anything, he grumbled to himself, but he knew how to deal with rats, coax 'em out with cheese then bludgeon their snarky grins with a hammer. He could shove their carcasses down the garbage disposal, and like his favorite old-time funny actor said, 'and no one will be the wiser!' Oliver Hardy never stuffed a rat down a sink, but he *did* own a gun or two.

What John Quincy would use the gun *for*, he didn't know, but he'd feel good just having one, and a reason might pop up eventually, he thought, he had a lot of enemies and he planned on making more. Like that Billy. He hated that sonofabitch, always playing pat-a-cake with Lexi behind the salad-counter. He *knew* Salad-Boy was bopping her, it was all over his stupid face, her stupid face, too, the slut. He wished he was a fly on the mattress of *that* bed!

That bastard-chef Ray wasn't exactly his favorite person either. Lately, wherever he turned, that buzzard was mean-muggin' him, like he expected John Quincy to pick up the whole damn kitchen and stuff it in his pocket so he could sell it at the flea market. Yeah, enemies were everywhere, his own snarky grin said, but just let 'em mess with me once, just *once*, I'll show 'em.

THIRTY-SIX

Lexi grew up in an upper-middle-class neighborhood and had *plenty* to show 'em. From the time she was ten, her mother was entering her in beauty contests and Lexi won more than she lost. Hair salons, make-up appointments, and seamstresses weren't cheap, but Dad could afford them, American Airlines paid their pilots well. But flying all over the world didn't leave him much time to attend contests. Mom was there, though, *boy!* was she there.

Little Lexi was prodded, nudged, nagged and cajoled up and down every contest stage and runway in the state. Mom quizzed, scolded, and pestered her until the girl had memorized every good answer to every question an emcee could ask: 'If you were God for a day, how would you change the world?' (Declare peace!) 'How would you end poverty?' (Give everybody a job!) 'Who is your role model?' (The President!)

Thru it all, Lexi smiled and glowed. Even when not parading down the runway, her hair was perfect, her make-up straight, her clothes spotless. She was elected junior high school class president, *twice,* was a four-year cheerleader in senior high school, was homecoming queen in both the eleventh grade and twelfth grade, dated the football team *captains*, yes, three of them, and received offers to attend nineteen different colleges. Then goody-two-shoes stumbled.

One of the captains introduced Lexi to marijuana, another to cocaine, and the other? To bourbon and blow-jobs. Her hair was often stringy now, her make-up smudged, her skirt semen-stained. But she knew how to get high and give a terrific blow-job, just not qualities an Ivy League University prized. Dad hinted there was always restaurant-management school, then climbed back into his cockpit. So after graduation and rehab, Michaelangelo's future assistant manager started her studies. Good fortune for Billy!

THIRTY-SEVEN

There are many types of fortunes. There's the money-fortune, there's the career-fortune, there's the love-fortune. There are billionaires, there are prime-ministers, there are Casanovas. Morty was none of these. *His* fortune was in lap-dancers, plenty of them. They came in waves, girls from broken homes, girls from juvie, girls from the street. They had one thing in common: they needed money, and fast. Whether it was rent, drugs, or pimps, each girl had a need. And Morty reveled in those needs.

Each dancer interview required an exhibition of talent, usually a hand- job, pole-dancing could be taught. What *else* did Morty keep the veterans around for, their sagging tits? No, they showed rookies how to convince a dreamer to stuff ones and fives in their red thongs, how to give a *special* fifty-dollar hand-job, one that would keep a satisfied customer coming back.

Some of the girls tried to hold out on Morty, hide the fifty under the perv-seat or even up their beavers. Morty knew *all* the tricks. He had the bouncer check under the seat after said customer left, installed a shower in the dressing room, demanding all girls at the end of their shifts rinse off, leaving any wandering fifty a soggy green mess. No, you had to stay on top of these bitches!

Morty could take or leave *any* of the lap-dogs, except one: Jenna was always his favorite, smart mouth and all, the best hand-jobber he'd ever seen. She'd made him more fifties than the next ten lappers combined. When she was on the floor, every perv with a fifty eating a hole in his stained overcoat pocket waited in line for *her,* and it could be a long line. When the bouncer tried to hustle a scofflaw out to the street, Morty had heard more than one refer to Jenna as *Hands,* like in 'Don't push me, tough guy, I'm waitin' on Hands!'

Lately business had been down, maybe the pocket-weasels had discovered another 'Hands' across town. Morty wanted Jenna back, needed those hands, needed those fifties. He'd never been to her apartment, but he had her address, and her phone number was on her unemployment application. It still bugged him that he'd let her talk him into telling the city she was laid off instead of quitting, *but* he had her number. Great city, they even paid the *lappies* for not working!

THIRTY-EIGHT

It *was* a great city! The morning after his odyssey thru the wormhole, Ray, for what seemed like the very first time, heard bluebirds singing on his way to work. He noticed flowers blooming as if for the first time. Brave happy-go-lucky sun had chased winter's sad clouds away. And for the very first time he felt wide awake, more conscious and more attune to the slightest sound. The scraping of a Japanese beetle scurrying across the sidewalk, the tapping of a cherry-tree branch against the deli window, the squeak of the church door as another sinner exited from confession.

Sure, he'd been madly in love with Jenna from that very first elevator meeting, but *this* was something different. No, not different, *better!* She'd shown him Shangri-la, Camelot, the Garden of Eden. They'd tasted the forbidden apple, drank from the Holy Grail, ridden the White Horse of Revelation, indeed, saw Heaven standing open, saints and angels beckoning them with out-stretched arms, enticing them to enter Nirvana.

Maybe Ray had never really known what love was before. It wasn't simply a warm body lying next to you, it wasn't simply an impulse to protect and suckle an appreciative mate. No, love was something more. A genuine, over-whelming hunger to touch every wish and dream and fantasy of another human being, to know their every thought, their every hope, their every prayer, their every *everything*.

Ray would never be the same again. He had touched whispered promises borne upon the wish-winged hush, bathed in kiss-stained love-light. He had reached across the breathless night to embrace a galaxy of magic stardust.

But a galaxy of magic stardust stretches only so far.

Part Three

THIRTY-NINE

The ring wasn't expensive, but it was real! When Billy had walked into Birnbaum's on West 47th, the bald security guard had yelled, "Hey, Jacob, ya gots a gee just come in!"

The bespeckled owner shuffled out from the back room in his flip-flops saying, "Baruch Haba! Baruch Haba! Welcome! Welcome! What can I do for you, young man?"

Motioning at the security guard, Billy asked, "What's a 'gee'?"

"Oy vey! Don't mind him, he's a *yutzi*, I only keep him on because he knew my *zayde*, thinks he's family."

"I'm looking for an engagement ring," said Billy, "my brother Ray got *his* here, said he got a good deal."

"Let me think, let me think, no, I remember no Ray."

"He's a chef at Michaelangelo's…"

"Ah, *yes, yes,* the *chef,* I remember now! Came in with Ahmad, my son's buddy. They went to restaurant-management school together. They've been, how does he say it, *best buds,* ever since. Who says Jew and Muslim can't be friends, *drek!* Although between you and me," Jacob whispered, "that Ahmad is kind of a *chutzpah!*"

"I don't know what that is, but it sure sounds like him," Billy laughed, starting to trust Jacob already, "you got anything nice but affordable? I don't have much to spend."

"Oy vey, I understand perfectly, young hearts are rich in love, not so rich in money. Ok, ok, let me see, affordable but nice. Ah, yes, yes, here we are, a real *ganeyve,* just came in yesterday," Jacob fibbed, reaching in and grabbing a tiny sparkling speck from a bottom shelf.

After gently wiping off the dust with his shmate, he set the miniscule diamond on a black velvet tray. "Stunning, isn't it? 1/4 carat!" Jacob informed Billy, handing him a loupe.

Billy examined the stone with the magnifying glass. "Kinda *dinky,* isn't it?"

"Once it's in a setting, it'll look bigger," assured the jeweler.

"I thought diamonds sparkled more, this one's sorta dull, and what are these spots?"

"That's called *clarity,* my young lover, every diamond has them, they're Mother Nature's birthmarks. Once the stone is in its proper setting, they'll be unnoticeable. So, what do you think?"

"I dunno, it's still kinda puny, got anything bigger?"

"Nit azoy ay-ay-ay, not that impressive, hey? Ok, ok, let me look," Jacob replacing the dinky diamond on the bottom shelf. "How about *this* one?' he said, bringing out the one right next to it, "beautiful, no?"

"Looks the same!"

"No, no, 1/3 carat, slightly pinkish tint, less inclusion. The pink is *very* rare, found only in the mines of Timbuktu," Jacob fibbed again. "In a 10k gold setting it will look *ravishing!* Do you know the lucky girl's ring size?"

Still unsure of the pink, the 10k or Timbuktu, Billy warily produced a mood ring that he had snatched off the salad-counter after Lexi had removed it to give him a hand-job the previous night. Ahmad walked by just as the 'lucky boy' had stifled his orgasm with a piece of romaine lettuce, and as Lexi hurried off, she hadn't even missed it.

"Yes, yes, this will do perfectly, such dainty fingers! She must be a real *zissele,*" exclaimed Jacob, "now where did I leave my mandrel? Ah, yes, yes, here it is, size 4, perfect! Leave a deposit and I can have this ready for you Friday, Thursday for an extra fee."

"Friday's fine," said Billy, feeling the lightness of the wallet in his back pocket.

"11am Friday," smiled Jacob, "11am. I even give you the *mishpocheh,* family discount for friend of Ahmad's. Mazel Tov, Mazel Tov!"

"*Yutzi,* get the door for the lucky groom!"

It isn't the size of the engagement ring that impresses a girl, it's the size of her beau's heart.

FORTY

They say size doesn't matter, but in guns, it really does. John Quincy wanted the biggest, baddest, silveriest pistol he could find. Well, maybe not silveriest, you could only buy so much glitter with $300. But he wanted the gun to be intimidating, like Dirty Harry's .44 Magnum. Again maybe $300 worth wouldn't strike fear in a perp's heart like a Magnum, but John Quincy still wanted *bad*.

He met his *guy* in a back alley off Chinatown. The street dealer's white van's rear doors were already opened up and ready for business, displaying Walthers, Brownings and Mossbergs for sale to two Mafia-looking Italians who were busy babyheading it over price. Although it'd taken him forty minutes and five subway stops to get there, John Quincy held back in the shadows. He'd been leery of Italians ever since watching re-runs of The Untouchables. I ain't messing with no Dago, he said to himself, "those ravioli-eaters is vermin". Robert Stack couldn't have said it better.

After the Italians left, John Quincy sidled up to the van, constantly looking over his shoulder expecting to see Popeye pop out with his hand-cuffs, saying, "I warned you, loser, hands behind your back!" It was ridiculous to think that goon knew what he was up to, he guffawed, but that dick *was* suspicious.

"You JQ?" queried the gun dealer.

"Me in person," said John Quincy, proud of his codename.

"Okay, chief, everything's five-hundred and up, get a move-on, I got an appointment at the U.N."

"Five-hundred? Spider told me you had $300 ones!"

"That was two years ago, boss, prices done gone up, inflation, thank the Republicans!"

"I only got three-hundred," said JQ.

"Well, kingpin, all you can get for that is a used one. Over here in the side door! They all work, just can't guarantee what they been used for."

JQ rummaged thru the used bin and picked out a Smith and Wesson ivory-handled .45.

"Good choice, governor, just like Patton carried. I give it to you for two-fifty."

Wow, just like General Patton's, *Old Blood and Guts* himself, grinned John Quincy, this'll impress *any* perv! He paid Van-Man and slipped the S and W into his overcoat pocket and began to walk away, singing, "Hi Ho, Hi Ho, it's off to war I go!"

"Hey, General, wants some fries with that burger?" barked the dealer.

"Whaddya mean?" asked the giddy ex-con.

"Bullets, genius, ya ain't getting' far in a career of crime on an empty gat!"

Thought I was going home with Patton *and* $50, John Quincy said to his disappointed self.

"How much?"

"Fifty dollars for the box, top cat, wrap it up to go?"

Great!, said the big war hero to himself, there goes one hand job!

FORTY-ONE

An engagement ring is a lot *like* a gun. You point one at a prospective bride and she freezes. As Billy knelt on the sticky floor at IHOP asking Lexi to marry him in front of screaming toddlers and old toothless men gumming their spinach omelets, it wasn't your most romantic of proposals, not of the Harry Met Sally-ish kind. There was no cabernet sauvignon, no Ozorio plates, no Christofle silverware, no rose smiling out from a Waterford vase, just Billy on one knee and a dumbstruck Lexi frozen like a deer caught in headlights.

"Lexi, I love you and I want to marry you, please say yes," proposed *Un-Harry,* "I know I don't have much to offer you yet, but I adore you!"

After several moments of just toddler screams and omelet-gumming and thoughts of *she doesn't want me* racing from neuron to panicked neuron inside Billy's flummoxed brain, Lexi finally drawled, "Snookums, I *like* you and all, honey bunch, but I'm not ready to marry, can't we just go on like we've been, sugar?"

Billy was crestfallen, and to make matters worse, one of the toddlers had hit him in the back of the head with a french fry and giggled, "Silly goose!" The waitress placed a check on the table, asking, "Will that be all?" Billy-boy's gloomy neurons, realists all, flashed inside his brain, *"And that's all folks!"*

It was a long, quiet walk back to Billy's walk-up. The flirting tree leaves still waved, the smiling stars still dreamed, the same brave guitar still sung out its message of hope from Luigi's Pizza Parlor. Only a commiserating Moon looked down in pity and summoned the tearful clouds to cover his face so he didn't have to stare at the anguish below.

As a miserable Billy followed Lexi into the apartment, softly shutting the door behind them, he mustered that slight wisp of courage crouching glumly in a darkened corner of his heart, whispering, "Will you be staying the night at least?"

"Sure, sweet cheeks, I don't work 'til ten," grinned Lexi, circling her warm summer arms around his icy winter neck, "nothing's *changed*, I'm still your girl."

FORTY-TWO

Everything changes! The seasons, the weather, the world's prospects. Respectful autumn changes to abusive winter, sunny day turn to stormy night, peace turns to war.

There was a war going on in John Quincy's mind right now, a battle between the autumned-forces of good and the wintered-forces of evil. He never wanted to find himself in prison again, *that* was the good-part talking, urging him to keep his nose clean and stay out of trouble. But then there was the idea of retribution, paying an ugly, unfair world back for cursing him with a drunk for a father and an addict for a mother. Getting even with this ugly, unfair world for putting a young, innocent him at the mercy of mean foster parents, leering pedophiles, and sleezy movie producers. And lap-dancing *sluts* who helped put an older, victimized him in prison. *That* was the evil-part talking.

So the neuroned soldiers in this war were constantly besieging John Quincy with arguments for-and-against. The *good* guys bought him chocolate bars and cigarettes, assuring him a better world was just around the corner, just on the other side of forgiveness. The *bad* guys bought him guns and bullets, cajoling him to 'fight the bastards', get even for every slap, every fondle, every lascivious peek at his underwear. Fuck forgiveness! Get even with every strip club bouncer, every book-stealing cell-bunkie, every corn-balling shower-wolf, every lap-dancing slut who had ever bad-mouthed him in court.

It may go without saying, the bad guys were winning the John Quincy War. The chocolate bars were lying in a ditch melting, the Patton gun was now his best friend, his *only* friend!

FORTY-THREE

Friends are best for one thing: warning you not to mess up. When Jenna called Cynane telling her Morty was offering to reward her handsomely for resurrecting her lap-dancing career, Cynane argued, "I don't care if he offers you the *moon,* honey, that scummy place is a perv-crawlin' flea-pit, and Morty's a lousy scuzzball who you should trust as far as you can throw him. And that ain't far, baby, the fat creep weighs three-hundred pounds now, you ain't seen 'em lately!"

"But Cynane, there's something I haven't told you, I'm pregnant. Ray hasn't had a raise in months, scummy landlord raised the rent, we could use the extra money."

All Cynane heard was the word *pregnant.* "Wow, Fertile Myrtle, you don't waste any time in the bedroom, do you?"

"Ray wants it every night," blushed Jenna, "I can't lie, I do too. But Cynane, the point is, my para-legal class is in the morning, that leaves my afternoons free. I can work afternoons at Morty's and still be home before Ray. He'll never know. I can use the extra money to fix up the baby's room and pay a few bills."

"There's a million better ways to make money, honey," Cynane responded, "when you left the business you were my hero, my *Great Girl Hope*. That a lap-dancer could escape the nastiness, the vileness, the *hideousness* of this nauseating life and hook up with a nice, decent guy was my inspiration. You're my inspiration, Jenna, my beacon of hope!"

"You never told me that. Are you getting out, too?"

"Not me, honey, I'm here for life, until my tits fall off. Where am I gonna go, what else do I know how to do? This is me. But it isn't *you*. Stay away. You got a good life now, don't fuck it up!"

"I'll think about it."

"If you come back, don't say I didn't warn you that you're fuckin' up. I hope I *don't* see you at the office, baby. Bye."

"See ya," whispered Jenna after Cynane hung up, tears forming in her eyes.

She *had* thought of taking up something respectable like nail-saloning or hair-styling or dog-walking. Then Morty called.

"Hey, baby dol', how's 'bout yu cummin' on ba'k? I's got yer ol' spot in th' dressin' room reserv'd fer yer swe't li'l ass! I's even gonna let ya ke'p ev'ry third fifty ya mak'!"

"Well *you're* a charmer, still know how to sweep a girl off her feet," Jenna had answered, meaning the exact *opposite*.

"C'mon, Angel, I's ain't gonna lie, bus'ness is in th' toil't an' I's ne'd ya. Th' ov'rcoats musta found a nu han'job'er someplace, cuz they ain't cummin' 'ere. No one left 'ere gives a han'job worth spit. Not lik' yu. I's ne'd thos' pervs an' their fifties ba'k an' I's ne'd sum han' bait! Whattaya say, baby dol'?"

"Wow, your sweet-talk never fails to impress me," she said, shaking her head as she clunked down the phone.

But it was a *job*, a job she could do right now. And it wasn't that hard. Dance a few titty-routines, slam-bam a few shrimpy dicks, pocket a few fifties. He'd said every third fifty. The chump, what Morty had never known is that she'd *always* kept every third one. That's what baggies were for, fifties in, seal the top, shove it back up the pussy, nice and dry when you get home. Now she would keep every *second* fifty. She had a lot of sandwich bags in the cupboard. That jerk, she said to herself, I haven't thought about this crap for months, one phone call and I'm thinking like a lap-dancer again, a hand-jobber! I hate it. I hate *him. Still...*

Needless to say, Cynane lost the argument.

FORTY-FOUR

Speaking of arguments, Cynane herself had recently had one with her boyfriend, Sammy. Well, boyfriend is not quite the right word. Sammy had been born a girl. Pastor Philipp had christened her Samantha Alice at Trenton's Saint Bartholomew's Baptist Church at the age of nine months, twenty-two years before she started hormone therapy for transition. When Cynane and Sammy met at Lar's Bar, Cynane was just coming off a lesbian relationship that ended badly, her girlfriend, Dee, leaving her for a female karate instructor. Cynane had surreptitiously followed them into a lesbian bar in the Village, secretly watched them dance the merengue, and after three gin and tonics, accosted them on the dance floor. Karate Teacher did a number on her, putting Cynane in the hospital for a week. Last Cynane heard, Dee and Karate were living down in Costa Rica.

Sammy had never had medical transition surgery, so still had all his female parts, which suited Cynane just fine. As a matter of fact, Sammy's lower parts were Cynane's *favorite* parts. In bed with the lights out, Cynane could fantasize she was licking Dee.

One night after sex, Sammy confided he wanted to fully transition to male. That's what started the argument, Cynane saying she didn't want a boyfriend with a dick. Sammy started crying, bawling Cynane didn't love him. Anyway, harsh words were said and Sammy ended up spending the rest of the night on the couch. In the morning, he was gone, clothes and all. He never returned and Cynane herself cried for two days, then resigned herself to the fact that boyfriends with or without dicks made poor substitutes for lesbians. Maybe there was a savior at that Village lesbian bar. No time like now to find out, she smiled. *Every* bar, straight or gay, probably had a savior.

FORTY-FIVE

Cynane always knew she was a lesbian. From the age of eight, anyway. Her single Army mom had named her after a half-sister to Alexander the Great. Princess Cynane had trained in the 'arts of war', was one of only three royal Macedonian women to lead an army into battle, and indeed, became infamous for single-handedly slaying the Illyrian Queen Caeria in 343 BC.

Growing up, Cynane never cared about princesses or dolls or any of the other 'arts of femininity'. Like her namesake, she liked action. Rock 'Em Sock 'Em Robots, Motorcycle G.I. Joe, Johnny West The Indian Fighter. At elementary school, she climbed the monkey bars with the boys while the girls played hop-scotch. But it wasn't the boys' climbing muscles that turned her on, it was the way the girls' dresses hiked up on their scotch-hops showing their thighs.

When she was in the fifth grade, Cynane was invited to a sleepover at her friend Zia's house. While taking part in the requisite pillow-fight, she tumbled down on top of another girl, meanly pinned her hands to the bed and kissed her.

The girl kneed her in the crotch and angrily pushed her to the floor, but that first kiss lingered on Cynane's lips for weeks. It was all she could think about. And around that same time, her fingers discovered that special spot between her legs as she fantasized at night under the covers about girls' hop-scotch thighs and pillow-fight lips.

By the seventh grade she had her own bona-fide girlfriend, Minh. They'd spend lunch hours in a rest-room stall sneaking cigarettes and making out. It was Minh who taught Cynane the Vietnamese tongue-twirl: gently tapping your partner's tongue-tip three times, pirouetting across the palate, pinwheeling from gum to gum, and after tracing figure-eights on the insides of both cheeks, finishing with a delirious and furious looping coil around your lover's tongue from the side.

Practicing the technique lunch hour after lunch hour made Cynane an expert kisser, which came in quite handy at future sleep-overs where the recipient didn't always knee her in the groin.

School year after school year, as mom and daughter moved from Army base to Army base, Cynane's lovers changed as often as the school restrooms. There was Laraine, "Call me *Larry*", (Ok!), Glenys, "I prefer *Glen*", (Got it!), Erica, "It's *Eric* to you", (Sure Thing!), Moesha, "Just *Moe*", (Nice!), Godiva, "Everybody calls me *God*", (What? No thanks!).

The lovers were great, not so much the school grades. Teachers don't grade on tongue-twirls. But then Cynane didn't care about school much anyway. There were careers that didn't need learning. That's what she thought. Wake up, girl, only job that doesn't need *some* education is erotic dancing, you don't even have to know how to dance! So, that's how she met Morty, a decent hand-job and she was in. Oh, well, she remembered thinking, there's no do-overs, when life gives you cherries, (How clever!), you bake cherry pies. She did.

FORTY-SIX

Jenna's cherry pie was Morty's. She planted her "swe't li'l ass" in her old spot in the dressing room and was stuffing more fifties up her beaver in one afternoon than a week of afternoons in the old days. Morty was so delighted to have her back on "han'-job duty" that he never even *mentioned* the baggie tuck.

He knew all about *that* ruse, he grinned, what did Jenna think, he's stupid? Thongs have been doing that since the beginning of lap-dance time, well, at least since baggies were invented! But she was worth the scam, business was up 30%.

He was making a lot more money, too. *"Hands is back!"* was spreading on the perv grapevine like wildfire. Pervs were coming out of the woodwork. Were they reproducing, Morty wondered, like pods in some science fiction movie? No matter, each pod came in with a fifty and left without one. That's capitalism at its best, he grinned, sell the customer something he's gonna need again and again.

For Jenna, her most *important* customer remained Ray, and her most important *duty* was keeping him from knowing she was workin' at Morty's. Her new motto: *Dash, Dash, Dash,* the three D's. She'd dash from class to the club, change into her thong, dash out to the floor, hand-job as many pervs as she could, then dash home to have dinner on the table by the time Ray got home.

All this hectic dashing would be worth it in the long run, Jenna reflected. She could already see herself as the legitimate career woman, doing para-legal work at a fancy law firm, raising a happy, loved child, and being a loyal and faithful wife to Michaelangelo's future head-chef. It was a great plan. What could go wrong?

FORTY-SEVEN

For Lexi, the three D's were *Derriere, Derriere, Derriere*. She loved women's butts. On the subway, at the grocery store, at the beach. Joggers, roller-skaters, cyclists. Jeans, peddle-pushers, yoga pants. For her, the world was a big wonderland of women's asses. Small ones, big ones, medium ones. The tight, taut, rounded ones were her favorites. When Lexi was walking behind one of these, admiring, sometimes a woman would feel her eyes and turn around, her stern glance saying, "Are you checking me out?" Lexi would just smile and then politely look away, returning her rapt admiration as soon as the woman turned back around.

Of course, Lexi liked men, too, hence Billy. Sometimes you just needed a cock. But the most excruciatingly beautiful sight in the world was a pretty girl. And for Lexi, she loved watching their backsides. She'd never really had the courage to proposition a woman yet, it scared her. Would that step make her a *lesbian?* Lexi hated labels, why couldn't you just be with anyone or anything that turned you on? Kiss and rub and lick your Paradises, your Utopias, your Elysiums?

Billy could never understand. Most men couldn't. That's why she'd never told him about her fantasy, her dream, her *thirst,* why she spurned his ring. She wanted the best of both worlds, male *and* female, Sturm *and* Drang, tempest *and* serenity. If the world *offered* both, then why not *take* both? Lexi just needed the bravery to make the move, the resolve to reach out, touch the other tantalizing, exhilarating, captivating half of the world she hadn't yet had the boldness, the temerity, the *guts* to embrace!

But Lexi was getting closer. Closer to tapping radiance on the shoulder, asking, "Can I have this dance?" Grazing up against temptation, saying, "I noticed you're alone, may I sit?" Savoring the woman's odor, sipping her smile, licking her loveliness. She would lead her amour to the dance floor, hug her emerald glance, caress her ruby sighs, confess that she needed, *hungered,* for a dream, a hope, a wish that would come true and *lift* her to Paradise on the wings of whispered love, where she would finally enter the heaven of satisfaction, touch the grace of intimacy, kiss the holy hem of sensuous salvation, penetrate the divine dimension of gratification, the coming together of *everything!* She was close.

FORTY-EIGHT

They claim close only counts in horseshoes. Billy had come *this* close to his own Paradise. He'd bought a ring, practiced his *I love yous,* even slapped some of that *Hai Karate* on his face that Ray had lent him. What went wrong? he asked himself. He was a good-looking guy, had a decent dick, knew his way around the bedroom. Apparently that wasn't enough for some girls.

He remembered this one dizzy bimbo he met at the canteen on the base. He was at the monthly 'Grab a Soldier and Dance' shin-dig, and this stacked blonde dragged him out onto the dance floor. He'd only had time to glug half a Coor's and usually needed at least three full bottles to get in the mood for twirling a hoochie around the pussy-pit. He couldn't take his eyes off that bulging sweater, those two cantaloupes were just begging to be slurped!

They ended up in some disco-dive down by the wharf, and after a slug of beers, Billy was ready to thread the needle, dust the dog, skin the sausage. They went back to her bungalow and Billy immediately went to work on those melons, slobbering over them like a gnat in a winery. He segued to her belly-button then on to her muff, logging in one of the most competent, enterprising stud-sessions he'd ever had.

Dog dusted and sausage skinned, he laid back and lit up a Chesterfield, a huge grin on his face. Mission accomplished, Captain, hill taken, victory assured. He puffed on his Chesty, and waited for his medal. And waited. And waited. The bimbo was over in the kitchen making a tuna salad, frown on her face, shaking her head.

Billy said, "How 'bout *that* performance? Do I get an Oscar or what?"

"Ya get the weenie award, *stud,* I didn't cum *once!* Who'd ya buy that tired screenplay off, an unemployed leprechaun who couldn't find a rainbow to save his pot-o-gold ass?"

Ego deflated and Chesterfield snuffed, Billy crawled back beneath the green mossy rock all out-of-work leprechauns live under and wondered, what do women *want,* anyway?

FORTY-NINE

What do women want? That question has mystified mankind for millennia. It was a long-held myth that Stone Age men hunted and women gathered. In the 1960's anthropologists concluded, some stubbornly, that in many cases, the sexes shared duties. It is no coincidence female anthropologists were among the first to assert that women were just as suited and capable to hunt game as men. And they did! Men were as equally prone to gather nuts and berries as women. And they did!

What do women want? To receive credit where credit's due! Men may rev the car's engine, but women lubricate it. And are just as capable of taking the steering wheel as men. Both Cynane and Lexi knew that they really didn't need men to engineer their futures, and destiny decided they should meet.

A lesbian bar is no different than a straight bar. Both serve alcohol, both attract lonely hearts hoping to meet other lonely hearts, and both have success filling those lonely hearts with hope.

Now hope can be a fleeting thing, lasting a night, an hour, a minute. But a night, an hour, a minute, may be more hope than a hoper walked in with. At times, everyone loses hope, fears the door has closed on happiness, aches for just one more chance at finding that edelweissed castle in the sky, at riding that golden unicorn under the rainbow. We wish to be loved, to be adored, to be *valued* for the intelligent, worthy, sensuous beings we are!

Luck is a gift. Fate just needs opportunity. What are the chances pipedreams align, shine on each other's heartaches, soothe each other's fears, fire each other's desires, warm each other's cold despair?

When Lexi worked up the courage to ride her unicorn, Cynane was there waiting, hoping to find her own castle in the sky. Eyes met, smiles touched, love shined. Fate just needs opportunity.

FIFTY

For John Quincy, fate is a hand-job. On the perv grapevine he'd heard that a lappie referred to as 'Hands' had taken up residence again at Morty's. Before he'd been introduced to dump-trucks and wolves, he'd only been to Morty's three times and all three times there was no one called 'Hands' on hand-job duty. His luck had never been very good. Almost two years had passed since he'd been bounced off the premises and he hoped no one there would remember him. That's the kind of hope that filled *his* heartache.

After he'd turned off the dishwasher and mopped the kitchen floor at Michaelangelo's, John Quincy tiptoed into the walk-in, moved the milk cartons, and reached into the rat-trap to feel his S and W. There weren't any rodents in the trap needing their skulls hammered, he was thankful for that, he was tuckered out. That stupid Mayor's fundraiser had sent a ton of dirty dishes his way. And tomorrow was a big day, his day off, and he was going to meet 'Hands'!

Last time John Quincy had graced Morty's with his presence, he'd been armed with only a penknife and everybody knows how *that* ended up. A pistol flashed from his overcoat pocket would chase the touchy-feely pervs away, no harm done, he grinned, besides no feel was worth a bullet. But don't let no muscle-bound bouncer fuck with him, the only muscles that could stop a bullet were Superman's. Hey, that was clever, he mused, he was feeling his oats tonight, wait'll 'Hands' gets a load of him. Tomorrow, three metro stops and a short stroll down the avenue would put him outside Morty's, just outside fairyland, one door away from Santa's Village. Twinkling neon lights would beckon him inside like a weary traveler coming home from a long road-trip, inviting him in to rejoin his waiting, loving family. And what family made a homesick voyager feel more welcome than a family of lap-dancers and hand-jobbers? This was *his* Paradise!

John Quincy would purchase a golden ticket and be pulled in to a fabulous storybook setting of hugs and smiles and wonders. He'd be home.

FIFTY-ONE

Hugs and smiles and campaign donations, that's what warms a Mayor's heart, especially the donations. Well, $1,000 a plate isn't exactly a donation, it's armed robbery, he laughed. But these big-wigs could afford it, he'd pay 'em back with favors, *that's* what kept this city humming, tit-for-tat, spit-for-splat, shit-for-fat.

Power's the main thing. Money's fine, but *power*, that's what kept *him* coming to work every day! Or was it *cumming*? he grinned. Power over average citizens' lives. Raising subway fares, increasing water rates, finding a loophole to defeat rent-control, making those deplorables, those despicables, those contempibles suffer! After they pay their taxes, who needs the repugnants? Maybe to unclog a toilet or cook a taco.

He didn't really *need* the $1,000-a-platers either, but he needed their money, *loved* their money! That's what kept him in Armani suits and Gucci shoes and supplied his wife with Chanel perfume! He couldn't afford those things on a mayor's salary, and he had to look his best, you had to look like money to attract money!

He couldn't afford yachts, he couldn't afford private planes, but he could *ride* on them. But he had to make the big-wigs happy to keep those invitations rolling in. They say there's a politician-heaven and a politician-hell, he chuckled, he didn't know who went where but he'd know people in both places. The journey's the fun part, the destination is unimportant, long as you have a good time getting there, and he was having a blast!

He brushed the Crème Brûlée caramelized sugar off his Armani lapel and headed for the pisser. Inside taking a leak, he had to stand next to one of those kitchen deplorables wearing a soup-stained apron and black hair-net. They should have their own bathrooms, he groaned, not be allowed to mix with the clientele.

As he strode out of the restroom without washing his hands, Ray said to himself, *nice guy!*

FIFTY-TWO

Someone said nice guys finish last! Leo Durocher or one of those other baseball oldies. Or maybe it was a football guy. Morty didn't care, what did he know about sports? What did he care about *nice?* No titty-club in the world was run by a nice guy. A titty-club's manager had one quality: he knew *customers!* And Morty knew customers. Knew them backwards and forwards, upside down and right-side up, sideways and longways. Morty knew the difference between a tourist and a local, a sports-coater and an over-coater, a guy out on the town for a little thong-thrill and a perv with sweaty hands in his pockets. The tourist came in with a stack of fives for thong-tucks, the perv sat in the back row wiggling his pockets and saving his stack for a hand-job.

Morty had seen it all. Groups of Wall Street types drinking like fish and throwing stock-swindle profits at pole-dancers. City Councilmen sitting next to two-bit gangsters and using the thugs' bribes to tip the lappies. Husbands on the lam from Jersey City gawking and gawping at body parts they hadn't seen in the trim since high school. Shy teen-age boys with fake

ID's getting their first look at a *real live* grown-up woman's foo-foo.

And the occasional women customers. They were Morty's favorites. Usually three or four came in together twittering and tittering, sitting up in the front rows smiling at the dancers, laying singles on the stage apron, not daring to touch thong nor g-string. These were his dancers' favorites, too, they smiled politely, paid for the show, and didn't paw the merchandise.

Ah, thought Morty, then there was the occasional single lady, his ultimate favorite. The fantasizing housewife, the curious business-woman, the lesbian who didn't know she was a lesbian yet. She might sit anywhere, front row, middle row, back row, but you could tell by way she walked in. She might tiptoe in, looking for an out-of-the-way spot where no one would notice her. She might stride in, an Amazonian Warrior setting up camp directly beneath the pole. She might keep moving place to place, either to get a better look or to move away from an in-coming perv.

And once in a blue moon, Morty would spy one of the housewives, eyes shut and tranquil mind drifting thru Xanadu, as a silky-soft, lily-of-the-valley perfumed dream girl slithered, slid and squirmed atop the fantasizer's libidinous lap. It was an adventure, a rapture, an odyssey thru wonderland, a pilgrimage to the far ends of the earth seeking serenity, grace, and the bliss of elatedness that the housewife could play over and over in her mind as she lay beneath her husband's stabbing, suffocating, crushing weight.

It was a scene that could last Morty a thousand unromantic lap-dog blow-jobs in his dirty, smelly, unblissful office. If only he *were* that lucky, dreamed Morty! The only lappie still giving him blow-jobs was Annabelle, and she was in Cleveland still trying to win a ballroom-dance trophy.

FIFTY-THREE

Trophies are awarded for Little League MVP's, bowling leagues' top bowlers, eating contests' champion hot-dog eaters, not for honesty. Still Cynane figured she deserved one for telling Lexi the *truth,* that she was an erotic dancer at a strip club. Lexi didn't seem to mind. It actually seemed to turn her on, as if she were bragging, "My new lesbian buddy takes her clothes off for a living!"

You take a big chance telling the truth about yourself, most people form opinions of you soon as they meet you. If it turns out they wanna see more of you, you don't just blurt out "by the way, I assassinate political leaders for a living", that kinda chills the whole 'hanging out together' thing.

Anyway, Cynane was glad she took the chance, if her and Lexi hit it off as lovers, that strip club info would've come out eventually and probably ruined everything. Better now than when they fell in love and got married. *Married?* thought Cynane, she hadn't even *kissed* the girl yet, put your dreams back in your heart, wisher!

Cynane knew she could do worse, though, remember that last disaster? she asked herself, *that* girl was a freak! She'd met Freak at Adele's Roller Boogieland, pierced eyebrows, scorpion hand tattoos, and a blonde shaggy bob with pink tips. Freak had skated up behind Cynane and patted her on the butt, saying, "I'd trade in my skates for *that* any day!" Cynane rather liked that.

The next time Freak passed, Cynane smiled and called out, "Offer still good?" Ten minutes and some small talk later, they were in the bathroom licking and flicking.

Cynane ended up staying at Freak's four-story walk-up for two weeks, most of their time spent squeaking and creaking the bedsprings until the next door neighbor would bang on the wall. Then they'd move to the floor and keep scissoring and fisting until one cried "enough!"

For Cynane, everything changed one night when Freak produced a velvet-lined pair of handcuffs, grinning, "Ready to play in the big leagues, honey?"

At first Cynane was curious. She'd fantasized about role-playing before, but this turned out to be more than just pretend. Freak turned savage, pulling whips and butt plugs out of her secret closet panel and suddenly becoming a snarling, vindictive punisher. Later when Freak unlocked the cuffs, fully expecting her slave to kiss her pain-goddess feet in glorious thanks, a silent purple-welted and tear-stained Cynane quickly grabbed her clothes, dressed and without looking back, hobbled shakily out the door and down the stairs to the 'safe streets' and never went back.

Lexi was different. She was the most demure girl Cynane had ever met. She didn't seem to have a mean bone in her curvy body. Her warm summer smile could melt a snowman. When they'd danced at the lesbian bar, Lexi's lily-pad pond eyes pulled Cynane's sore soul into their caressing ripples and drowned her in emerald serenity. Lexi's hair smelled of vanilla and raspberries, her whole *aura* promised days of rainbow-lit laughter and nights of moon-lit wishes. Maybe Cynane didn't *have* to put her dreams back in her heart.

FIFTY-FOUR

Ray had a dream he was standing in a wasteland of bones, Jenna's warm rescuing smile nowhere in sight. Sun and clouds overhead danced a twisted minuet, there was no sign of life, no birds, no trees, despair stretching far as the eye could see. He wandered the soulless, godless desert searching everywhere for his wife, his lover, his friend, trying to retain a picture of her shining face in front of him. But as he trudged on thru the hollow, ruined landscape, her image slowly faded into nothingness, into blankness, into numbness. He was alone, a weary and dreamless ghost tumbling into the void of a black hole.

Suddenly he was a snake slithering across a moaning beach underneath heartbreak's smoldering sky, weeping clouds beginning to pain-rain on his writhing, whimpering snake-body, his snake-head losing all memory of Jenna beneath the scorching noise of the dream-bursting thunder. A huge crashing wave pummeled and *pulled* his snake-body into a screaming, scarlet sea, shattering his snake-head and obliterating any possibility of Jenna ever existing again.

No longer a snake, Ray dreamed he was sitting in a lonely bedroom overlooking Fifty-Seventh Street. The lemon-sherbet moon was sinking behind a tall, half-finished skyscraper, dawn-shine just beginning to chase the night fog away. And in the dull morning twilight, faceless and nameless people passed by his tear-streaked window. They couldn't see him, they couldn't feel him, they couldn't heal him, and somehow he knew it'd be no different tomorrow, no different the next day, no different forever. He reached out to close the curtain, out there no future existed, out there no Jenna existed.

FIFTY-FIVE

Existence is a slippery thing. Do you know you exist because someone *loves* you? Do you know *they* exist because *you* love *them?* Or does the entire acknowledgement of both of you that you must *both* exist depend on the pain, anguish and despair you both suffer when apart?

Billy missed Lexi. Missed how her smile made flowers bloom, missed how her glance made trees wave, missed how her voice made stars twinkle. Ever since Lexi met Cynane, she'd been avoiding him, though as yet, Billy didn't know they knew each other. He'd only himself met Cynane *once,* at Ray and Jenna's reception, never knew her circumstances, he didn't care, didn't find her attractive at all.

Funny how the world turns in silent denial that lovers are fated to stay together, always introducing new and enticing temptations to their existence. Lucky temptations that make them turn their backs on a lover that titillated their every fantasy, tantalized their every dream, abandon all that for a fresh intimate who penetrates and satisfies their every *idea* of what existence should mean.

Billy didn't know luck from fate. He did know anguish and despair and pain. The pain of losing the best thing that ever came his way, the finest smile, the lushest glance, the sexiest voice he'd ever welcomed into *his* existence.

After bidding a now unromantic Lexi good night at Michaelangelo's, Billy would head home to his dreary flat. Dreary because Lexi wasn't there to make it glow, make it shimmer, glisten with hope, hope for the future, the future of all sparkling existence.

When shimmering love abandons you to dreary despair, anguishes you to an existence of godless deserts and scarlet seas, then you think love will never fate your desolate road again, never luck your lonely path anew, never tempt your existence *to* love.

Shimmering love had abandoned a lot of Morty's customers. What teen age boy sets out to be a strip club junkie? Teen years should be years when a boy learns about all the gleaming opportunities for love, from secret notes passed to him in class by the messenger of an admiring female, to flirting smiles inviting him to explore the wonders of a first kiss beneath the high school bleachers at halftime.

Hesitation is a boy's worst enemy. Lingering too long in the shadow of indecision to meet a flirter's enticing gaze, he watches in horror as the flirter is spun around by a braver and bolder suitor, never to look the poor lingerer's way again.

Jenna profited off the lingerers who never left the shadows, dawdling-boys-turned-to-dawdling-men fumbling into Morty's in their overcoats to dream and fantasize about opportunities missed, still afraid to meet a woman's gaze, even a lap-dancer's.

Sitting in the back rows, fondling their fifties with one hand, kneading their hard-ons with the other, they waited for not a flirter, for those opportunities were long gone, but for a pretend lover with a baggie up her beaver.

FIFTY-SIX

What John Quincy needed right now was a hand-job. Those self-wanks at home were good but a woman's soft, delicate palms felt better. He glanced around Morty's theater, a few suits in the front row, nine or ten pervs scattered around, not a bad crowd for a Thursday. There was even a single lady in the fourth row. *That* might get interesting, he thought, if he got lucky he might see a free woman-on-woman lap-dance. What was best though, was that he didn't recognize one face in the place, not even the burly bouncer's. That meant no one would recognize *him*, important, he nodded, since he'd been permanently 86ed from the dive. Hard to enforce an 86 if no one remembered you.

He took a seat in the same row as Single Lady, he didn't want to be too far away when *that* show began. There were two thongs shimmying and shammying on the pole, sliding their high-heeled ankles against each other's thighs. Three or four lap-dogs were working the audience and since each rub-and-grind took anywhere from five to twenty minutes depending on how long a guy's 20's held out, John Quincy would just have to wait his turn. In the meantime, he reached under his overcoat and started a wiggle-tempo to keep time to the pole-dancers' entwined ballerina-spins.

Morty peeked out from his office and smiled. He'd have a slew of twenties and fifties to deposit in the bank tomorrow, even minus Jenna's baggie stash. At this rate, he'd get to retire to the Maldives five years early. He smiled again.

Jenna was making the rounds. She preferred dealing with suits, they paid with fifties, not with crumpled up and fives and tens. But today, they were all sitting in the front row, and Morty had one rule: no hand-jobs in the first three rows. When the occasional undercover came in, he only looked for monkey-business in the front rows, what went on in the shadowlands was fair game. Even the occasional undercover occasionally graced the shadows! So Jenna did slips-and-slides on perv-laps, her least favorite laps. Why is it every perv had bony knees? It made her beaver hurt, she complained to herself, maybe they needed more calcium in their diets.

And each time she took sweaty money and sat down on a bony knee, joggling and wabbling a perv into la-la land, Jenna would close her eyes and dream of the future.

Ray had recently told her that Ahmad had heard the owner say he was thinking about promoting Ray to dinner-chef. Anson had been burning the salmon again. Surely the promotion would come with a big raise and she'd be able to gather her baggie-fifties and tell Morty to *shove it,* that her lappie and hand-jobbing days were history, a horrid, hideous past *blasted* to oblivion. She and Ray would decorate the baby's room and plan for a rapturous and radiant future! She joggled and wabbled and smiled.

Cynane was on lap-dog duty that day too. Even though it cut down on her pay, she tried to avoid hand-jobbin', that part of a customer's gear was her least favorite. She could take the sticky, clammy hands creeping and crawling across her shoulder blades while she slipped-and-slid, and the hot, foul, revolting breath on her neck, but she hated touching the pervs' lizards. Morty had scolded Cynane repeatedly, saying, "Ya w'rk 'ere, ya gotta do th' 'hole job, t'uch th' liz'rds, they ain't gonna bite!" But he always relented and kept her on, she'd been the best slip-slider in the joint, and he knew it. More of the $20 pervs waited for *her* than anyone else.

When Cynane spotted Lexi waving at her from the fourth row, she hurried over to her, completely ignoring a glasses-wearing nurd thrusting his hand toward her clutching a soggy, wrinkled ten and two moist, crinkled fives.

After inviting Lexi down to the club to watch her pole-dance, Cynane didn't really think she'd show up. A girl like Lexi didn't grace strip clubs with her presence. She attended operas and symphonies on the arms of hedge-fund managers and grocery-store magnates. Yet here she was, with a smile that glowed with breathless trust, confident that no matter how dingy and dirty the surroundings, how squalid and sordid the terrain, Cynane would never let anything bad happen.

Cynane perched on Lexi's lap, facing her honey-faithed upturned lips, breasts brushing breasts, thighs tickling thighs, fingertips petting finger-tips, until tongues reached out for each other joining in satiny, velvety kiss.

This was gonna be good, gloated John Quincy, boy, did *I* come on the right night! His right hand was *thumping* under his overcoat, if he didn't slow down, he'd cum before the hand-job! Wait a minute, he suddenly halted himself, I *know* that girl. The slut from Michaelangelo's, the one who'd never given him the time of day!

"Wanna party, stranger?" John Quincy looked up and at that moment, all the demons in hell smiled at him. It was the *bitch* from the courthouse, he'd never forget her accusing face. He pulled his right hand out of his wet overcoat pocket and leaped up off the seat, his other hand clutching the Smith and Wesson. The demons had indeed smiled at him, bringing together in one room at one time his two arch-enemies, the two *skankholes* who haunted his half-house dreams!

Bullets are *made* for arch-enemies: the Mexican weasel sneaking thru a hole in the border fence looking for a better life, the black trouble-maker marching thru the hood protesting yet another act of police brutality, the welfare queen complaining on TV that her precious food stamps have been cut again; they all hafta die, pay the price for daring to think this corrupt world should be a better place, daring to think that, if only given the chance, they could help change things for the better, daring to assume they have a God-given birthright to expect to live in a fairer world, a nicer world, a world minus the racism, minus the inequality, minus the hate!

Filled with seething rage at everyone who had ever hurt kids like him, mothers who prize meth over their own children, fathers who prefer liquor to raising their sons, foster homes that expose unwanted kids to pedophiles, movie producers who film naked children for the sick enjoyment of perverts, John Quincy pointed his weapon at Jenna and fired. An earth-shattering thunder-clap sprang out of his gun-barrel of retribution, filling the strip club with panic as patrons and employees ran for the exit.

John Quincy spun around and pulled the trigger again, a bullet entering Lexi's forehead, killing her instantly. Cynane *screamed* in terror as blood spurted onto her face, her overwhelming reaction to flee overcome by her fierce need to protect her new-found lover from further harm, shielding Lexi's body with hers. Protection was her last thought on this unfair planet as John Quincy aimed his vengeance at the back of her head and fired.

At the first gun-shot, Morty hid under his desk, yanking the cord on his phone until it came tumbling down onto the floor. His trembling hand dialed 911. Police responded within minutes.

The last thing on John Quincy's mind was fleeing the zone of retribution. He had three bullets left, three shots to quench the rage still coursing thru his veins. He looked around for other do-gooders who thought the world should be a better place.

Finding none, he headed toward the red *Manager's Office* sign. Flinging open the door and seeing a leg sticking out from beneath a desk, he crossed the room and took aim. As a bullet entered the back of John Quincy's head, his last thought was *fuck the world.* The police officer advanced, kicked the Smith and Wesson away and lowered his weapon.

Part Four

FIFTY-SEVEN

"Mr. Mayor, any comment on the mass killing taking place at a strip club today?"

The Mayor stared at the reporter with annoyance, replying, "This was *not* a mass killing. The federal government defines mass killings as three or more people."

"Three people *were* shot," responded the reporter.

"Only two died, one's in the hospital," said the Mayor, "next question."

"Any comment on the gun restriction bill being considered by the legislature?"

"My only comment is guns don't kill people, shooters do."

"There wouldn't be any shooters if there weren't any guns."

"That's all I have time for, this press conference is now over!" grumbled the Mayor.

FIFTY-EIGHT

"The bullet penetrated the right frontal area of the brain and was lodged in the right occipital lobe. We have performed a pterional approach and decompressive craniectomy to reduce intracranial pressure. The foreign object has been removed. Unfortunately, the patient has not emerged from the coma she entered the hospital in. Trying to predict when she will regain consciousness is problematic. All we can do is wait."

"We were able to deliver her fetus, but regrettably the baby died due to its limited gestation period. If the fetus had been older than twenty weeks, it would have had a stronger chance of viability."

"Can you tell me what sex the baby was?"

"A boy," replied the surgeon.

"A boy. I was going to have a son." Ray gulped.

Finding Jenna's student body card in her purse at Morty's had led the police to call the school where her college application listed Ray as next of kin. He stared at the surgeon, praying these doctors knew what they were doing.

Ray had been staggered when the admitting nurse had informed him that the ambulance had picked up his wife at a downtown strip club called Morty's.

"A strip club? No that's not possible, you must be mistaken, can you please check the records again? My wife's information must have been mixed up with another patient's. Jenna's a college student on a leave of absence from a law firm, studying toward an advanced degree. She's never been to a strip club in her life!"

The admitting nurse examined the paperwork again. 'Patient in room 303 picked up at Morty's Strip Club on W. 38th at 1:47 PM. Admitted 2:07 PM.' "There's been no mistake, sir."

As Ray was listening to the nurse, his mind was saying, "No, Jenna was *not* at a strip club!"

"Can I see her?" he asked the doctor.

"Certainly," said the surgeon, but she won't be able to respond to you."

Quietly pushing open Jenna's hospital room door, Ray took a seat next to the bed. She was wearing a respirator and tubes were connected to both arms. Over the soft beeps of a machine, he could hear her shallow breathing. He had no idea if she would be able to hear his voice, but he had to *believe* she could.

Taking her hand, he whispered, "Jenna darling, I'm here now, and I will never leave your side. You'll be up singing and dancing again in no time," and again he prayed.

Ray had never spent much time with God. He'd attended Sunday School only once. A hairy-legged Puerto Rican girl he had a crush on in fifth grade convinced him to go with her. But the teacher's lesson had gone right over his head, all those stories about an *Infallible Father* and *His Sanctified Son* passing down poetic parables to mortal men to speed them on their jagged journey to redemption.

As he got older, he'd watched televangelists claiming to be the messengers of God, beacons lighting the way for His ever-eager, faithful-faced flock to embrace His gossamer gospels with wonder-waiting arms. Preening prophets beckoning followers to baptize their weary souls in God's wisdom-winged words. And always ending their canons with promises of soul-saving salvation in exchange for ample remuneration.

Could the *Infallible Father* and the *Sanctified Son* be both taintless truth and farce? Ray couldn't take any chances either way, he needed both *Father* and *Son* to be real *now*, needed every bit of help they could bless Jenna with.

"The doctors say as soon as your brain heals, you'll be on the road to full recovery," Ray whispered, not knowing if this was true, but knowing optimism is the healer of all traumas. Lightly holding her hand, he hoped this optimism would penetrate Jenna's skin, enter her veins and arteries and ride the platelets to her brain, circle thru her heart, and somehow find her essence, her atman, her being, giving hope to every molecule of her body, every atom of her soul.

Later that evening, the door pushed open and Billy and Ahmad slowly and quietly walked in. Billy pushed a chair closer to Ray and sat down clutching Ray's hand.

"How is she?"

Squeezing his brother's hand, Ray answered, "The doctors say she's stable."

"I spoke to the owner, Ray," said Ahmad softly, "he said to tell you to take as much time off as you need."

"Thank you."

"I wish there was something I could do," whispered Billy, "people feel so helpless in these situations."

"Pray for her, brother, pray for her."

"I don't understand what they were doing in a *strip* club," uttered Billy, as he sipped his tasteless coffee in the hospital cafeteria. He searched Ahmad's eyes for an answer that could somehow untangle the mystery of why both Jenna and Lexi had gone to a venue that cost the love of his existence her life.

"The world turns in mysterious circles," replied Ahmad.

"What kind of an answer is *that*," glared Billy, "more Muslim *bullshit?*"

Before Ahmad could be offended, Billy apologized, "I'm sorry, I didn't mean that."

"I know, son," understood Ahmad, "anguish makes even the best-intentioned of men intolerant and contemptuous at times. Perhaps your god has a reason, all gods do."

FIFTY-NINE

Ray reached into the bag of clothes he'd asked Billy to bring him. Inside was a small mirror and a razor. He removed them and set them on the nightstand. When Jenna awoke, the first sight he wanted her to see was his freshly-shaved smiling face.

Four days had passed and Ray had not spent *one moment* away from his wife's bedside except for five-minute showers in the adjoining bathroom. He'd arranged for nurses to bring him meals from the hospital cafeteria and refused to leave the room to speak to doctors, insisting they come to him.

Hope is eternal he assured himself. He would wait here until Jenna awoke, until the earth stopped revolving, if that's what it took, until the stars stopped shining, until all other life on the planet vanished. The woman in the bed was the only lifeform that mattered.

Hope!

"Dear, when you're feeling better, we'll rent a car and drive back to the Columbia River Gorge and stay at that little cabin overlooking the lake. Maybe take a hike around the lake, get your walking legs back."

"Then when we come back to the city, we'll look for a bigger apartment, something near the park, buy some bikes, go riding 'neath the cherry trees. There's so much we haven't done yet. I want to take you to museums, Broadway shows, to the top of the Empire State Building, to the beach, hot dogs at Coney Island."

It's so easy to let the joys of life pass you by, to forget what's important, what's crucial to making our time on this earth count. Smiles, kisses, walks in the rain, holding hands while watching the ruby sunrise. Showing your soulmate there's nowhere else in the universe you'd rather be than in their arms. Tears filled Ray's eyes.

He hoped, he *prayed,* that he and Jenna would have the time to do all these things. *Time,* the most important ingredient in life. Without enough time to experience all the beauty of just being alive, then a life is wasted. Maybe not wasted, but shortchanged, like a ride on a streetcar that only travels one block, the conductor calling out, "End of the line, folks, everybody off." What'd'ya mean *off,* I just climbed on!

Time. Time to see everything. Time to do everything. Time to share with your true love the magnificence of life, the majesty of snow-covered mountains, the pageantry of the nighttime stars parading thru the heavens, the spectacle of a dream-shimmering moon rising over the fate-sparkling ocean horizon, the friendly merriness of the tinkling aspen leaves. All this and more. Much more.

SIXTY

Ray closed his eyes, he was feeling drowsy, he hadn't slept in days. He quickly reopened his eyes, struggling to stay awake, he refused to give himself the luxury of sleep when his wife, his lover, was lying in a coma in a hospital bed, perhaps screaming inside, "Help me, I'm here, let me out!" Was she pleading, "Ray, save me, pull me back from this precipice of silent eternity, this abyss of forever-frozen winter. Save me! *I wanna come back!*"

He pushed the nurse call-button, hoping she could bring him a cup of coffee. Suddenly the monitors started beeping, red lights were blinking off and on. What had he *done?* He panicked, not knowing what to do.

The door flung open, two nurses rushed into the room, one quickly pushing buttons on the monitors, the other checking Jenna's pulse.

"What's happening?" screamed Ray.

The doctor on call sprinted in. "Pulse, nurse?"

"No pulse, doctor."

The doctor grabbed defibrillator pads. "Charge! Clear! Again! Clear! One more time! Clear!"

The doctor slowly backed away and set the pads on a table. He looked at Ray, shaking his head, "I'm sorry."

A nurse removed the respirator and pulled a sheet over Jenna's face. She glanced at Ray's horror-stricken face, then looked away, walking out of the room.

The other nurse said softly, "Sir, you'll be more comfortable in the waiting room."

"*Comfortable?*" his insides screamed, "my wife just *died!* I'll never be comfortable again!"

In one *moment* his entire world was gone, fate had shut the door on every entryway to happiness, hope had reneged on every promise of contentedness, the *Infallible Father* and the *Sanctified Son* had turned their backs on him. The good life was a *myth,* a *fairy-tale,* a hallucination unfurled by bogeymen and hobgoblins.

"Sir?"

"Can I have some time with my wife, please?" he whispered.

The nurse looked at the doctor and he nodded, "Take as much time as you like. We'll be outside. Come out when you're done," and they shut the door behind them.

Ray walked to the bed, removed the sheet from Jenna's head, and stood staring down at the most beautiful face he'd ever seen. How had this happened? Where was *Time?* Where was the lifetime together they were guaranteed? There *are* no guarantees in life, sucker, mouthed the imp grinning mischievously on his shoulder.

He glanced at the razor on the nightstand. Reaching over, he extracted the blade from its holder. As a sad sun dropped below the horizon, Ray lay on the bed next to his wife, his left hand lightly stroking her cheek, nestling his nose against her ear, still astonished that he'd had the privilege, the blessing, the *gift,* to spend a brief part of his life with splendor, with bliss, with a *miracle,* for that's what Jenna was to him, a miracle.

His right hand fingered the razor blade, it would be so easy, so simple, to cut his wrist now. It made so much sense. What would life be without Jenna, what would be the point of existence without her, of going thru all the silly tedium of living in a world void of the one thing that gave him hope, gave him strength.

Sweet memories washed over him, one by one coalescing in his mind: Jenna running for the courthouse elevator, her high heels chattering across the wood-paneled floor singing out an aria of summer-dreams; he and Jenna strolling arm-and-arm down an elm tree smiling 51st Street, a coconut-sherbet moon sighing in approval of two lovers' trust in silver destiny's lyrical wisdom of bringing together a pair of promising young passion-pilgrims.

Happy memories of Lake Gillette reflecting sunlight-glittering emerald diamonds on a bedroom ceiling as Jenna's honeymoon love-making transported him in feverish ecstasy to the edge of the blissful beyond; Jenna standing naked before him, water-droplets clinging to her shimmering loins, inviting him to sip the tulip-dew of her enchanted forest. That was all gone now, lost, forbidden to him, only the memories survived. But memories are not enough to keep a man alive.

He was so exhausted. The razor blade slipped from his hand, tinkling to the tile floor as he fell into a deep sleep, the slumber of a million happy memories, a million happy embraces, a million happy kisses.

Ray dreamed Jenna was standing on a shining hill, her outstretched arms reaching for him, summoning him to join her. He started to run, then spread his arms out like wings and his feet left the ground as he soared toward his lover. They met in glorious jubilation, melting into each other's kissing souls in unifying harmony, together vaporizing into exultant euphoria.

The stars above them beckoned and they arose in spiraling passionate wonder, the planets encircled them, comets streaking them to the edge of the galaxy, where time stopped, where ruby and emerald meteor showers guided them thru swirling clusters of magenta dust clouds and whirling vermillion gases to the mouth of a gigantic, shifting, seething wormhole where together they disappeared into its spiraling, writhing, undulating safety.